REBUILDING FOREVER

A SMALL-TOWN SECOND CHANCE ROMANCE

ANA RHODES

Stardust Publishing LLC

CONTENTS

AMBER

*T**hree months ago...***

I worked my way carefully over the patches of ice, silently willing warmer temperatures to come through Palmer. The snow was a treat during the holidays, but when it lingered into March, I got sick of its "magic".

Plus, the ice and the overcast sky took on an even more ominous feel today as I worked my way over the frozen patches of grass to the fresh grave in Union Cemetery.

It felt like the whole town was at the funeral and even though I might have been able to go undetected amongst all the people, I stayed away.

Patrick Murphy, a pillar of our small community, had unexpectedly passed away the week before. One of his poker buddies got worried when he didn't show up for his weekly game and found him at home in the recliner.

The town doctor said it was a heart attack. I hated the idea of him dying alone at home, but I was grateful it was quick. The last thing I wanted to imagine was Patrick suffering.

Standing before his grave, I said a quick prayer and placed a rose on top of the new tombstone. Liam had done an excellent job—it was simple but tasteful, something Patrick would have liked.

Chills went up my spine knowing that Liam was somewhere in Palmer. Until today, I had the comfort of knowing he wouldn't be coming back here. When he left thirteen years ago, that was it. No visits, no phone calls... just gone. Patrick would fly to Austin a few times a year to see him, but Liam had meant it when he said he was never coming back to Palmer.

I tried not to focus on that. The heartache he caused still hurt, even after all these years. I feel like I've lived an entire lifetime since then. I've been married and divorced and am now raising the most amazing daughter I could ever hope for. Today isn't about our teenaged love gone awry. It's about the man finally resting in peace.

Patrick and I had stayed close over the years. It had been difficult at first—I couldn't see him without thinking about Liam. But he was all by himself. Liam's mom died when he was a baby and it had always been just the two of them. Once Liam left, I felt bad knowing Patrick was wandering around that big old house by himself.

I made a habit of saying hi when I saw him around town and eventually, when I started my baking business, I always made a little extra for Patrick. He was my unbiased taste tester. He would tell me when something worked, or it tasted awful.

We had only gotten closer since my ex-husband left. I think he felt bad Abigail didn't have a dad. Although it's not like I ever had one, so I guess I kept up the family tradition on that one.

Patrick stepped in as a grandfatherly figure to Abigail. He even dressed up as Santa the last few years and tiptoed around the front porch so Abigail would catch him with his large velvet sack slung over his shoulder.

I would forever be grateful to Patrick for that. For a time when I was younger, I thought Patrick would become my family, but all that changed when Liam ran off. When I came back to Palmer after my divorce, Patrick was one of the first people to welcome me home with open arms.

I wish I could say it was the same with everyone else in town, but he was one of only a few who stepped in to help. We had an unspoken agreement that discussing Liam was off the table. There was no question about who had ended things. When Liam decided to leave, I'd begged him like a fool to stay. It's a memory that still makes my face burn with embarrassment.

But Liam evidently meant what he said about needing to get out of Palmer, because once he left, he was gone for good. When Liam eventually settled in Austin and Patrick would go to visit, he'd asked me to check on his house to make sure nothing was amiss. When he returned, he would say his trip was "good" sparing the details of how Liam was. I appreciated the gesture.

Maybe it was silly of me. It had been thirteen years since Liam left, and we were kids. But there are moments when it doesn't feel like all those years have passed. When it didn't feel like I'd survived a marriage and a divorce and had already gotten a child out of diapers. There were moments when I closed my eyes and I could still feel the thrill of excitement that raced through me at the touch of Liam's fingertips skating down my skin.

That touch had felt like home to me then, and in my more vulnerable moments, I could admit to myself it still did. That was back when I believed that every touch was a promise for the future, which made all of his little touches even more exciting. It didn't matter that we would struggle. It didn't matter that we would never be rich. I didn't care about any of it, even though my mother had voiced plenty of concern over it. No, it thrilled me to endure whatever struggle was necessary if it meant Liam and I would be together.

I shook my head free of my thoughts. Now was not the time to reminisce about an old love, especially one who had betrayed me.

I focused my attention on the grave marker before me and made a vow to Mr. Murphy: "I'll make you proud, Patrick. What are we going to do without you? I would've brought Abigail, but I didn't think she was ready. Thank you for supporting me when others didn't and for stepping in when you didn't have to. I will always love you for that."

I looked down at the bloom in my hand, a single white rose. I don't know why, but it seemed like the most fitting one for Patrick.

Swallowing around the lump in my throat, I placed the rose on top of his marker and stepped back, swiping at the tears streaming down my cheeks.

I started to turn away when something stopped me. I hadn't done it before because I thought it might be silly, but I decided to go for it. I dug into my bag and produced a little cardboard bakery box.

Inside was Patrick's favorite flavor of cupcake: chocolate brownie, with caramel ganache and extra sprinkles.

I sat it down next to the rose. "Here you go, one for the road."

That's when my emotions overwhelmed me and I hurried away, barely seeing through the blur of tears.

I was in such a rush, I almost slipped on a patch of ice, but I caught myself. It was in that moment I stopped to look around. I was certain I had been alone in my conversation with Patrick, but I couldn't shake the feeling that someone was watching me.

I looked around the abandoned cemetery. Nobody in sight, just me and the sound of my ragged breath.

I looked back at Patrick's grave. Maybe it was him, I thought to myself. Maybe that was his little tap on the shoulder, telling me to be careful as I crossed those icy patches. It seemed like something he would do.

But as I got back to my car and made my way home, I couldn't shake the feeling of being watched. It had to be my imagination getting the better of me.

For the first time in years, Liam Murphy was nearby. That I could feel his presence so keenly everywhere just reminded me how awful the heartbreak had been. It cut deeper than signing the divorce papers from my ex-husband.

But today was about laying Patrick to rest, not reminiscing about Liam, I reminded myself.

It still didn't seem real that he was gone. Just a week ago, Patrick stopped by the house to tell me the latest recipe I dropped off was going "to be the one." Of course, he always said that. He would try out my recipes with a relish, and then swear up and down it would be the one to catapult me to business stardom.

In fact, he was the one who encouraged me to think about getting a storefront. My mother was against the idea, telling me the upkeep would be too much for me as a single mom. But Patrick disagreed. He promised as soon as I got enough money together to open my store, he'd help me with whatever repairs needed to be done or appliances installed.

The cupcake had been my daughter's idea, and I made it with a flavor combination he had suggested the day before he died.

I should've checked in on him more, I thought to myself. I should've made sure he was taking his meds. He had a heart defect his whole life. The local doctor said he had a pretty good run, considering he'd been carrying that around all these years. But that gave me little solace. It seemed unfair that somebody so good and kind didn't have more time on this earth to enjoy the town he loved so much.

Patrick had been the town's local carpenter for years. It never made him rich, and sometimes he struggled to put food on the table, but he was easily the happiest person I knew. He'd grown up in these mountains. He knew how to hunt, exactly what plants to stay away from, and what could sustain an empty belly for a while.

Liam's mom had died during childbirth. It had always been just him and his dad. While I knew Patrick missed his wife Molly more than anything, he never got down about it.

He told me he didn't have time to be depressed about it because he had a baby to take care of. He said he got a blanket and wrapped it around him the way he'd seen his mother do with his many brothers and sisters. Then he fashioned a little baby Bjorn, strapped it to his chest, and carried on with work.

"I'm sure it was an OSHA violation, but I never let him too close to anything that might hurt him. And that boy could swing a hammer properly before he could walk," he always reported proudly. And he'd been right about that. Liam was just as handy as his father and seemed destined to follow in his footsteps.

But that had been a sticking point for my mother.

I hated her for it back then, but now, as a single mother, I can understand her concern. My dad left when I was young, leaving my mom to figure it all out, and we struggled. She resented him for that and always told me I needed to make sure I found somebody who would take care of me.

She didn't see that in Liam Murphy. She didn't see people who foraged and scrounged as innovative and self-sufficient. They were poor and the last thing she would ever allow was sending her daughter off with some poor boy.

I still have some anger in my heart over that. Because for all of her advice to find a husband who could "take care of me", here I was a single mom, just like she'd been, struggling to make ends meet. Mama figured I'd hit the jackpot when I married a law student. It never occurred to her that even a rich husband can leave his wife and child at a moment's notice—with nothing.

For all of her fussing about Liam, it sounds like he did pretty well for himself in Texas. I don't think he was rolling in lawyer money, but he had a roof over his head, and was doing just fine. Not that it mattered. I wasn't interested in any man's money. I was only interested in caring for my family and making sure my daughter and I were okay.

I hadn't realized it at the time, but Patrick's presence provided stability for Abigail and myself that was gone now. I wondered if I could pull this off without his gentle, guiding hand.

A few days after the funeral, Abigail and I were bustling out the door, running late as usual to get her to school, when Abigail squawked out my name that made me jump out of my skin.

My heart started pounding, as most parents do when their kids make that sound. "Abigail, what's wrong, baby?"

Abigail was pointing to our porch railing. There, right next to the finial, was one of my white bakery boxes. It was the same one I'd left on Patrick's grave marker. Abigail had drawn a picture on the outside and wrote a message for him.

We looked at each other with wide eyes, and then I shook my head and hurried to the railing.

Gingerly, I picked up the box. It was lightweight now—the heft of the cupcake was gone.

I threw a reassuring smile over my shoulder at Abigail and opened the box. Indeed, the cupcake was gone, a couple of chocolate stains on the edges of the box remained, and a note folded neatly in its place.

I plucked the piece of paper out and unfolded it. It was shaking in my hands. It read in a familiar handwriting, "Thank you for the cupcake. That flavor is a winner, don't forget it. I love you always."

"Mommy? You're crying. What does it say?"

I quickly swept away the tears and assured Abigail they were happy tears. I read the note to her, and she looked up at me, confused as I rushed to explain, "I think Patrick wanted you to know he loves you and he's watching over you."

I wasn't sure if that was the right thing to say. I often felt that way as a parent, but I was rewarded with Abigail's serene smile and her steps seemed to pick up a little as we walked to the car. She had a million questions about where Patrick was and what he must be doing, and I tried to answer them as best as I could. But when I kissed her goodbye for the day, my mind immediately went back to the familiar handwriting on the note.

I'd seen that handwriting on a hundred notes, all proclaiming their love.

I shook my head. I doubt Patrick kept it a secret he was close to me and my daughter. And I'm sure from the drawings on the sides of the box, Liam understood somebody would be missing his dad almost as much as he did.

It was such a Liam move. His dad would have been proud—reaching out to console a little girl who he didn't know.

And even though I knew that was all it could be, I couldn't help but feel haunted by the words "love you always."

Once upon a time, Liam had promised me that very thing, but it wasn't enough to make him stay. He shot out of this town like a cannon the first opportunity he got, leaving me in the dust.

I bolstered my resolve with that reminder. He'd made a kind gesture to a little girl, and it was sweet, but it didn't change that he had run away from me.

LIAM

Three months later...

It's never too late to say you're sorry or that you made a mistake. And it's not a bad thing to change your mind. Sometimes what's right in the moment isn't right forever, so don't let your pride get in the way...

Those words of Pop's had been bouncing around in my head since I laid him to rest. It still felt a little serendipitous that I'd even found his note. It wasn't a letter per se, but more of a list. While I was staying at his house planning the funeral, I'd run across a list entitled "Things I need to tell Liam."

My Pop was known for his lists. He made them for the grocery store, games he wanted to remember to watch, for idle comments said during chit chat with various people in town, and apparently, he made them for things he wanted to say to me that might be more difficult.

That had always been a tactic of his. He told me once he started the lists because he had such a hard time remembering everything he needed to know once my mom died. I never knew her, but they had a great love between them. Both of my parents, from what I understood, had been super capable, just in different ways. So my dad didn't know what to do with the little baby he'd been left with. He knew how to frame a house or fix a fence, and he could coax just about any animal into submission. But as he told me, he was out of his league with the squalling, angry bundle of joy he had to care for by himself.

When my mom died, a lot of the women in town flocked to Pop to help with the baby, and each one had their own set of instructions and advice for him. Pop struggled to finish high school, but he was an avid student of life, and he took copious notes. That's when the lists began. He didn't want to miss out on anything that might have even the slightest potential for importance later on.

I had mixed emotions about every list I'd found in that house, but I tucked this one away in my wallet behind a picture of Amber I'd never had the heart to take out. And I knew, without a doubt, she was the person he was referring to. He'd been trying in small ways to push me toward Amber ever since I'd left.

My first few years in Texas, I was stubborn and still convinced by Amber's mother's words to think there was any option other than to leave Palmer.

Sandra, Amber's mother, was fiercely protective, and understandably so. She'd never had an issue with me growing up, but that all changed when I started dating her daughter. And when Amber and I talked about forever and the life we were going to build together, Sandra didn't hide how she felt about it.

She was the one who convinced me I couldn't be enough for Amber and I bought it hook, line, and sinker.

But as time went on and life unfolded, I questioned the intelligence of the young man I once was. In a way, Sandra had been right. I was an idiot to believe her—and not believe in myself and what I was capable of. I was more than enough for Amber.

Then Pop told me about the guy Amber married. I remember thinking he must've been Sandra's dream come true. He came from money, and that was exactly what she wanted for her little girl.

But as I started hearing about the demise of Amber's marriage, I started coming to terms with the fact that I screwed up. The problem was, it was too late. We weren't kids anymore with our whole lives ahead of us. I couldn't come crashing back into her life, especially now that she was a mom.

So Pop kept dropping hints as he talked about Amber. I told him in no uncertain terms it was too late, and I would have to learn to live with it. He would drop the subject temporarily and bring it up later in the conversation. I knew they were close the last few years, and I was grateful for her presence in his life. At least he had somebody looking out for him.

"Dammit, Liam," I muttered to myself as I ran a frustrated hand through my hair. It's a phrase I've been muttering a lot lately. After all the ways I hurt Amber, I couldn't face the pain of going back to Palmer and Pop's. He always came to me, but I should've swallowed my pride and visited him as often as I could. I never imagined I'd have so little time with him.

I was still trying to make sense of it. Pop had a heart defect, but he was as strong as a bull and healthy as a horse. At least, that's what the doctor told him. He took his meds, and he watched what he ate. None of this made sense to me.

And if the shock of losing him wasn't enough, going home after over a decade to the place where I could feel Amber everywhere had been a serious mind fuck.

I spent my time half hoping, half dreading I'd run into Amber.

Thousands of scenarios ran through my head about seeing her, but none of them involved eavesdropping on her talking to Pop at his grave.

I couldn't make out what she was saying, and I didn't try to. That was a private moment between the two of them. I almost blew my cover when she slipped on the ice, but she recovered herself, and I forced myself to stay hidden in the shadows.

I had to smile when I saw what she'd left behind. The rose was one thing—but the bakery box with a cupcake inside, that was Amber for you—always thoughtful, always unique.

When I picked up the box and saw the childishly written note on the side from Abigail, I smiled. I'd heard quite a few stories about Abigail, and according to my dad, she was a miniature version of Amber.

I hadn't wanted to hear about Amber or her new family at first. Any time Pop would bring them up, I would change the subject, telling him about something that happened at work or asking him for advice on some carpentry issue. But then, about three years ago, when I tried to dodge the subject again, Pop's voice had turned harsh. "Now dammit Liam, you need to listen to me. Amber is not in a good way right now. That no-good husband of hers is gone, and it's just her and Abigail. Word around town is Abigail's dad left nothing to help, so now Amber's in the same boat as her mom growing up, trying to make ends meet off of nothing."

I remember being flabbergasted by the news, along with a mix of other confusing emotions: worried, relieved, vindicated, but mostly heartbroken. It all seemed like a stupid, tragic love story now, and for what? I consoled myself with the knowledge that she got the safe life her mother wanted for her. She deserved to be happy and taken care of.

Now it seemed terribly unfair. Amber would be every man's dream wife, not one to be abandoned to figure it out for herself—the very thing Sandra accused me of being likely to do. I never would have left her... except I did.

I didn't leave her with a kid, and I didn't break up a marriage, but I was guilty of breaking promises and breaking her heart. I wasn't sure if I would ever forgive myself for that.

When I dared to open the box left on Pop's gravestone, the sweet smell of chocolate instantly assailed my nostrils. It was such an odd thing to be enjoying in the wake of everything that happened that morning. After I listened to all the beautiful words said about my father, I had to deliver a eulogy myself, all the while trying not to bawl like a baby. Now here I was standing at the foot of his grave, inhaling the sweet smell of a cupcake made by the very hands I had turned away from thirteen years ago.

I wasn't sure what to do with it. I figured it probably wasn't a good idea to leave it out for the animals to eat.

Just then, the wind kicked up and blew through the first buds on the trees, where droplets of ice were clinging to the bright green. I looked up and saw a couple of doves roosting on a tree branch, burrowing into one another, trying to stay warm. I had to laugh.

When I was younger, my dad taught me to hunt. It was considered a rite of passage for most young men in the town of Palmer. I wasn't a fan, but he insisted, so we went bird hunting with one rule: never shoot the doves. He said they were my mom's favorite because they mated for life, and she didn't want to have the responsibility of stealing somebody's mate, so he left them alone.

I tore my gaze away from the doves and looked at Pop's marker. I took the birds as a sign of what to do with the cupcake in my hand.

I smiled at the cold stone before me. "Well, Pop, seems a shame to let it go to waste, so I'll take one for the team," I joked, even as tears ran down my face.

The first morsel that hit my tongue caused an explosion of flavors. This didn't surprise me. I'd enjoyed all of Amber's baking in high school, and she had clearly improved tenfold with time.

It tasted so good. This whole situation was ludicrous. I was sitting at the foot of my father's grave, chowing down on a cupcake made by the one that got away. I burst out laughing, which quickly turned to tears.

"I don't know how I'm supposed to do this without you, Pop. I don't know to walk this earth knowing you're not here, without you being a phone call away."

I lost track of time, sitting there crying like a child, but it was a long time judging by the numbness of my ass, and I had quit feeling the cold. Once the tears finally stopped, I focused on the message on the side of the bakery box.

In dark blue crayon, there was a sketch of a stick figure that looked like a man holding the hand of a little girl. Next to it was a note that said, "This isn't goodbye, because you'll always be in my heart. Love, Abigail."

So here I am, wandering this earth without either of my parents, with this list my dad had made of things he needed to tell me, and the loving note of a little girl I have never met who was being raised by the only woman I ever truly loved.

I needed to get the hell out of Palmer and back to my life in Austin.

When I returned to Austin, I tried to lose myself in my work—I had plenty to do. I was the CEO of a very suc-cessful construction company. I had people pulling me in fifty different directions and normally I let that consume me, but when I came back from Pop's funeral, none of it seemed to matter anymore. No matter how hard I tried, the urgency in my business partner's voice sparked little urgency within me.

I kept thinking about Pop, and Palmer, and Amber.

For the last three months, I'd been distracted, exhausted and couldn't figure out what to do with myself.

When I moved to Austin, it was because I heard there was plenty of work to be had. I didn't know at the time we were going to build a multi-million-dollar empire. My business partner and I enjoyed many years of expansion along with Austin's population boom. We had more work than we ever dreamed of. In a blink of an eye, Murphy & Torres Custom Builders went from fortunate newcomers in the housing market to the top choice for designing luxurious properties.

If anyone asked me or Benny, it didn't feel like it happened overnight. We worked our butts off and hired good people who produced high-quality work. Once our business was successful, I think a lot of my work ethic came out of vengeance. Sandra had convinced me I could never provide for the woman I loved and yet here I was, employing hundreds of people at one of the most reputable real estate companies in Austin.

I never let on to anyone back in Palmer how successful I had become. My dad knew, of course, but he was such a quiet and humble guy, he didn't see the point of boasting about his wealthy, successful son. He told me on multiple occasions he was proud of me, and that was enough.

I thought it was going to take an act of Congress for him to agree to let me cover the expense of expanding his house. He hadn't wanted to at first, but when I showed him the plans our architect had drawn up, making the porch wrap all around the house and putting in a sunroom, I could tell my dad was excited. Apparently, he and my mom had plans when they bought the house to expand it, and now it was coming to fruition. Still, my father admitted to me that when some people in town asked how he could afford the addition, he'd mumbled something about having "savings for a rainy day" and left it at that.

There'd been plenty of times I'd fantasized about waltzing back to Palmer with my newfound wealth and shoving it in the naysayer's faces, but then I would think about Pop. He was so proud of how we'd thrived off of what little we had.

There was a knock at my office door, and then a head popped in. "Hey, I got your text. You wanted to see me," Benny said as he moved into my office.

I looked at the man I started all this with, my best friend, and I felt a pang of guilt about bailing on him, even if only for a short time.

"Yeah, have a seat," I said, gesturing to the chair in front of my desk.

Benny plopped down in the chair across from my desk, looking worried.

"I wanted to talk to you privately about something. Do you think you'd be okay holding down the fort if I take an extended leave of absence?"

He looked surprised. "I guess... how long are we talk-ing about exactly?"

I shook my head. "I need to get things buttoned up with my dad's house and settle his estate. Frankly, I don't know how long that's going to take."

There was a quiet and thoughtful silence for a long moment before he asked, "Is that all it is?"

I looked at him strangely. "Yeah, what else would it be?"

He gave me a knowing smile. "Could it be a certain girl back home?"

Before I could stop myself, I corrected him, "She's hardly a girl. We're both in our thirties, and she's got a kid now."

Benny's eyebrow rose in a way that told me I was trying to fool the wrong person. "And? She's not married anymore. She was close with your dad until his death. There's a lot of history up there for you, man. You can't tell me it's as simple as packing up your dad's house, selling it, and then coming right back here. Can you really walk away from where you grew up and all those people you care about that easily?"

"Are you trying to talk me into giving up the business or something?" I laughed.

He leveled me with a serious stare. "I'm worried about you, my friend. You've been throwing yourself into work ever since your dad died, and I understand that, but it's obvious you're not okay. If you need to take extended time away from work, take all the time you need. I'm not worried about that. I'm worried you're trying to run away from your feelings."

I rolled my eyes at him. "Since when did you get all touchy-feely?"

Benny looked at me, slightly annoyed. "Come on, man. Don't do that thing where you act like you can't deal with your emotions because you have a dick."

I glanced to the floor and back at him. "Has Evie been making you listen to those woo-woo self-help podcasts again?"

"Ha-ha. You can make fun all you want, but there's nothing wrong with being a more self-realized individual. That's all right," he said flippantly, waving a hand at me, "you keep acting like the tough guy who doesn't have any feelings, and see how far that gets you."

There was a long silence before I relented. "No, you're probably right. I'm sorry, man. I'm not running away—I just don't know how to deal with this. It's not like I had to process my mom's death in the same way—I never knew her. But my dad, he's been my person my whole life and now he's just... gone."

"I don't think we ever get used to somebody being gone. We find a way to live with it. And if we're being honest, you and I both know it's not just losing your dad that has you all riled up. There's another reason you've stayed away from Palmer."

I shook my head at him. "Remind me to never get drunk with you and spill my guts ever again. Would you let it go?"

"Look, it's just you and me in here. It's not like I'm going to spread tales to the other guys. You have nothing to be embarrassed about. There was a woman you loved, you fucked up big time, and you feel bad about it. I mean, it's been thirteen years..."

"Exactly. It's been thirteen years and we're not kids anymore. We built completely different lives a thousand miles apart. What do you suggest? I go talk to her like nothing ever happened?"

Benny shrugged. "That's not what I'm suggesting and you know it. Maybe just talk to her. I mean, you said it yourself, you're both adults. So you should be able to talk to one another without it being awkward."

I shook my head. "I don't know, man. I did not leave on good terms. Besides, I need to get my dad's affairs in order and wrap things up. There's work to be done here."

"Hey, I can handle whatever we have going on here. It took me a long time to come to terms my mom's death, so if there's anything I can do to help you recover a little faster, you let me know."

I smiled at him. "Thanks, man. You're a good friend."

Benny gave me a wide smile. "Damn straight! Now I need you to do one thing for me when you get settled in."

"Name it," I told him.

"Every time your dad came down here, he'd tell me about these delicious confections Amber would make—I need to try one. There's this Trix flavored buttercream cupcake. I gotta get me some of that!"

"I'll see what I can do, but I'm not making any promises."

Truth be told, I had absolutely no intention of getting a cupcake for Benny. I would do nearly anything for my best friend, but tracking down my ex-girlfriend whose heart I broke so spectacularly when we were kids to satisfy his craving for a cereal-flavored cupcake? Yeah, that was a no dice situation.

As Benny and I hashed out the details of my absence, I tried to focus, but my mind kept straying back to Amber. Maybe my dad and Benny were right. It was time to face my feelings and make amends with the woman I'd done wrong.

Amber

"**A**bigail Grace! Put a move on it, we're late!" I hollered down the hall for the umpteenth time. It seemed like déjà vu because we did this every school day. Oddly enough, on holidays and weekends, Abigail would be up and ready to go at the ungodliest of hours.

I threw her freshly packed lunch bag into her backpack and made sure she had her homework folder.

I made sure she had the essentials. The last thing I needed was a call from school saying she forgot yet another thing.

I couldn't blame Abigail—she was as scatterbrained as her mom and the last few months had been especially hard. Losing Patrick after he had become such a special part of our lives affected Abigail deeply. We talked a lot about how his spirit was always here watching over her.

Personally, I remained saddened by the void Patrick left, but I was equally disturbed by the knowledge that Liam had been in Palmer. He must have gone back to Austin right after the funeral. I would have run into him by now if he had stayed. But lately, every corner I turn has me worried I might run into him. Perhaps it's just wishful thinking?

Now that's silly, I told myself. My obsessive thoughts about him since the funeral are bordering on ridiculous. I have a child to raise, and a business to run and yet memories of Liam have sprung loose and I can't seem to put them back in the box no matter how hard I try.

I was still a child when Liam left. So why do my memories of him feel more real than the memories of Abigail's father? I have no delusions of my ex's affect. His absence is apparent—not because I miss him, but because he has provided little support to ensure Abigail is well cared for. It all rests on my shoulders and while a part of me prefers that, there are moments like this I wanted to scream out in frustration.

But I don't. I stuff it down, put a smile on my face and I hug my little girl goodbye and try not to worry as she skips off to school with her Moana backpack bouncing against her back.

Thankfully, we were only a few blocks from school, so we could make up the time if we were running late. I waved to Abigail's teacher and hurried back to the car to move out of the drop-off lane before the honking began. Drop-off parents could be quite aggressive.

I had to get moving, anyway. I had to put the finishing touches on a novelty cake for the pharmacy on Main Street.

I make a variety of desserts for everything from baby showers to work parties, but I've become known for these uniquely sculpted novelty cakes. Today I will put the finishing touches on a cake in the shape of a pill bottle. The prescription label listed the owner of the pharmacy and the prescription read, "Take some much-needed time off. Thank you for fifty wonderful years."

I muttered and cursed to myself as I tried to accomplish everything in my tiny kitchen. I still think about the storefront Patrick kept encouraging me to open. There is an empty shop on the corner of Main Street that would be perfect. Abigail and I drive by it nearly every day and she always points at it and says, "Look Mommy, there's your future bakery." She and Patrick were my biggest cheerleaders.

When I mentioned the idea to my mother, however, she'd pursed her lips, do that humming thing in the back of her throat before clucking her tongue and saying, "Amber, sweetheart, I don't want to see you get your heart broken again."

My mother was always certain I was on the precipice of certain heartbreak, whether it had to do with Liam or my business ideas. The only person or idea she'd been fully on board with was my ex-husband. He'd been a law student, after all. He was going places, no doubt about it.

Only after a year of marriage, he dropped out of law school. No big deal to me. I wanted him to do what made him happy. He proceeded to bounce around, never really settling on a career while I worked my butt off.

He had come from money, so all he had to do was gripe to his parents about how money was tight, and the next thing I knew, they were wiring us money. I supposed I should've been more grateful, but I found it more stressful than anything else. I was working two jobs while he was still "finding himself." And things only got more stressful once Abigail came along. I absolutely adore my daughter but I wasn't able to keep my second job once I got into my third trimester, and this forced my ex to take a job he didn't want. He was certain it was going to kill him. I didn't see what the big deal was. He got a job easily as a car salesperson, and he was pretty good at it. That sales gig kept us afloat for several years.

Then one day he came home and told me he couldn't do it anymore. I tried to reason with him and I told him to take a break, that it would all work out. But he said he needed more than a break—and the job wasn't the only thing he couldn't do anymore.

He was gone by nightfall, and a huge part of me was relieved. But soon I would learn he had no intention of remaining in his daughter's life. So we moved back to Palmer, and I started this business out of my kitchen in the hopes I could spend more time with Abigail and eventually make better money than I had been.

It has been a struggle, and it's made worse by having to explain to Abigail where her dad was, because honestly, I didn't know. His mother reached out occasionally to check on Abigail, so I knew he was safe, but he was clearly not interested in being a father.

I carefully boxed up the cake, loaded it into the back of my car and then I slowly drove up Main Street with my hazards on. Palmer had grown used to me driving like a granny, so I would not jostle my cakes.

The pharmacy was ecstatic about the cake.

"Amber, you have done it again! This is perfect," the manager of the pharmacy said enthusiastically. "How soon do I need to get on your schedule for a Christmas party cake?" She asked in all seriousness, and I had to laugh.

"Considering it's only July, we have a little time, but I appreciate you thinking of me."

From there, I was off to take a much-needed trip to the grocery store. Not only did I need to fill in the cupboards for Abigail and myself, but I needed more baking ingredients, so a significant portion of the check I just received would go to the groceries.

I started at one end of the store and worked my way aisle by aisle, scoping out everything and trying to remember what I needed. I really need to make a list. My neighbors were used to seeing me looking harried in the aisles of the supermarket.

I still had on my yoga pants and a baggy t-shirt I threw on that morning, something I could spill cake ingredients all over, and my hair was tied up in a messy bun. I'm sure I had bags under my eyes. I had gotten little sleep the last three months, tossing and turning, thinking about the ghost of boyfriends past.

My cart was half-full, and as I raised up on my tiptoes to grab the shortening off the top shelf, a familiar voice sounded in the next aisle that almost had me drop the can of shortening right on my face.

"Well, you're a sight for sore eyes. I didn't see you after Patrick's service. How've you been, buddy?"

I froze, trying to listen over the thudding of my heart in my ears. Then the familiar voice sounded again, smooth and deep.

"Yeah, I'm back to take care of Pop's house."

"You're going to be selling his house?" The other voice asked, and I bit my lip, willing myself to hear better.

"Yeah, it's not doing anybody any good sitting empty. Someone should enjoy it as much as he did."

The other person clucked their tongue. "Well, it's going to be really hard to imagine anybody else in that house other than your dad."

The voices lowered somewhat, and I couldn't quite make out what was being said, but it sounded like they were moving. Panic tore through me and I threw the shortening in my cart and looked around wildly to see which direction was the best way to go.

"Shit, shit, shit," I said under my breath, as I spun around and headed to the opposite end of the aisle, pushing my heavy cart like I was in the Olympics. I screeched to a halt at the end of the aisle and craned my head out, looking both ways to make sure I was in the clear. Satisfied that I might have escaped, I steered the cumbersome cart to the right, and almost ran smack dab into the denim clad crotch of a very tall form.

"Oh my God," I squealed, as my eyes rose from the point of near contact up the muscular chest to the square jaw of none other than Liam Murphy and his shocked expression.

"Amber," he breathed. I could feel myself turning crimson down to my toes.

What was that thing my mother was always nagging me about? To put a bit more effort into my appearance, because you never know who you will run into in public? I always replied that I didn't particularly care. Anyone who couldn't handle me at my worst didn't deserve me at my best.

But standing there in my yoga pants and ratty t-shirt, with my messy hair in front of Liam Murphy, was one of the few times in my life I wished I had listened to my mother's advice.

"Um, hi," I said lamely. "Wh-what are you doing here? I mean, not in the grocery store, but, in Palmer?" I sputtered out.

Good God, what happened to my ability to talk?

He smiled. "Oh, uh, I'm here to tie up some loose ends with dad's place before I sell it."

I just nodded because what did I say to that? I had to agree with whoever he'd been talking to on the other side of the aisle—I couldn't imagine anybody else in the house but Patrick. It was the end of an era that was much too painful to consider. And this was one of those moments when I wished Patrick was still here because he would tell me what to do and how to handle his son.

"Right. That makes sense."

"It's really good to see you, Amber," he said.

I looked down at my disheveled appearance and raised an incredulous eyebrow. "Oh, sure. Tell me, have you been stuck on a ship for several months?" I asked him sarcastically before I could stop myself. And then Liam did something I didn't expect after all these years.

He laughed. I hadn't heard that laugh since I was eighteen years old. I had forgotten how deep and hearty it sounded and how it touched me deeply, like a much-needed warm hug that always made me feel special.

It had been so long since I'd felt special.

That realization sent me panicking again, and I gave him a timid smile and said, "Well, I should pay for this and back to work. I have a lot to do before I pick up Abigail."

"Right. Pop told me about Abigail and how awesome she is," he said, shifting nervously from foot to foot.

I smiled wider this time. "Well, he's right about that... was right about that. Damn, I'm still getting used to saying that," I said, glancing down at the pile of food in my cart.

Liam nodded. "Yeah, I keep finding myself picking up the phone to call him for one of our daily chats... then I remember."

I couldn't stop what I knew had to be a sorrowful expression, because despite everything that happened between us, I couldn't imagine the pain he was going through. Hell, I was struggling not being able to talk to Patrick. I can only imagine how hard it was for his own son.

"I'm sorry for your loss, Liam," I said quietly.

"Thanks, Amber," he said, looking at me in a way that was all too familiar, and I couldn't handle it.

"Well, um, I should be going."

He moved out of the way, noticing he was blocking my path. "Right, maybe I'll see you again sometime?"

Was that hope in his voice?

"Um, yeah, maybe," I said, moving past him and shoving the cart towards the checkout line.

My heart was beating like I'd just run five miles and I couldn't help but look over my shoulder. When I looked behind me, he was watching me with a puzzled expression—he looked a lot like what I felt.

Come on Amber, I chastised myself.

I was in my early thirties, had an eight-year-old daughter, and a mountain of worries I had to climb every single day. Yet here I was, locking eyes with my high school sweetheart, my heart racing like I was sixteen years old again.

I couldn't shake the feeling there was more he wanted to say, but he just kept watching and finally I tore my gaze away when the cashier asked, "Amber? Are you ready to check out, hon?"

I put my attention back on the cashier. "What? Oh, um, yeah, I'm sorry. I've lost my head today."

"What kind of wild and wonderful art piece are you going to be baking up next?" The cashier asked me, having checked me out through many of my baking adventures.

I tried to remember what my next project was and make small talk about it—and attempt to focus on the pleasant woman in front of me and not let my eye stray to where Liam had been. "Um, I uh, I'm making a cake for the Johnsons' anniversary party. It's their fortieth."

"Their fortieth? Can you imagine?" The cashier asked.

I shook my head. "No, actually I can't," I laughed.

The cashier smiled at me. "Neither can I, sweetheart. I usually tolerate each of my husbands for about three or four years, but then I can't stand them anymore and have to break up. Some of us just aren't made for forever," she said with a wink.

I knew she was trying to make a joke and relate, but it still stung. I'd been all about forever until Liam abruptly left, and it made me rethink everything I ever thought I understood about the world.

It wasn't like I hadn't made a concerted effort with my ex-husband, and Lord knows I tried everything I could. But even then, something in me knew it wasn't in the cards.

Maybe the cashier was right. Forever just wasn't in the cards for people like us.

As I left the store and pushed my cart through the automatic door, I kept my eyes glued forward. No surreptitiously looking around to see if Liam was nearby. I wondered if he was still watching me as closely as he had been a few minutes before.

I thought I did a fine job of acting like everything was perfectly normal as I threw the grocery bags in the trunk of my car. And only after I settled into the driver's seat and closed the door did I heave out the breath I hadn't realized I'd been holding.

How the hell did that hurt from thirteen years ago become so fresh in the blink of an eye?

"Get your shit together, Amber. You don't have time for this. He's in the past, and that's where he needs to stay."

But even I could hear the shakiness in my voice as I said the words to myself. I was no longer a single mom in the middle of a shopping expedition, shaking uncontrollably in her car. Suddenly, I was eighteen years old again, reliving one of the most agonizing conversations I've ever had with the person I loved the most. I was shaking then, too, and sobbing, wondering how the hell I was going to move on.

Only now I knew exactly how I would move on. Thirty minutes from now, a very sweet little girl would be waiting for her mommy to come pick her up from school.

I sucked in a deep, cleansing breath and pulled out of the parking lot. I rushed home to unpack the groceries, losing myself in the routine I performed a thousand times. While driving to school to pick up Abigail, I reminded myself that my daughter was the one who mattered. Not the destitute deadbeat dad who wasn't smart enough to know when he had a good thing. Not the mother who was never happy with anything I did. And definitely not an ex-boyfriend who stomped my heart to dust.

No, my entire world was waiting for me with her cute little Moana backpack, and that's what I needed to focus on... not the devastatingly handsome man I once knew.

LIAM

P ain. That's what I saw in Amber's eyes after all these years.

I wasn't sure what I had expected to see. But what I'd seen flash in her eyes had me fighting not to fall to my knees.

Thirteen years. It had been thirteen years since I'd left this place and her behind, but it felt like it happened the day before.

Despite all that, Amber was as sweet as ever, even though she hurried to get away from me as fast as her feet and her cart would allow her.

I watched helplessly from the entrance of the grocery store as she quickly piled all her stuff into the trunk of her car and climbed inside like somebody was chasing her.

"Fuck," I muttered to myself as I strode out to my truck and climbed into the driver's seat. Maybe this had been a bad idea? Maybe I should've had some local lawyer take care of the sale of Pop's house.

I tapped my fingers restlessly on the steering wheel, wondering how much of a chickenshit I would feel like if I just went back to Austin now.

I reached across myself for the seatbelt, and the action caused a rustling sound from my shirt pocket. I didn't have to inspect it to know what caused it: Pop's letter. The one telling me it was never too late, the one that encouraged me to make amends no matter how painful.

Yeah, I was going to have to muster the strength to face Amber again—no matter how much it terrified me.

I wondered what possessed me to even go into the grocery store. I'd just arrived in town and instead of going straight to Pop's house, I stopped off at the store first because I had a hankering for a bag of chips.

I never got that bag of chips. I slowly followed Amber across town until she turned off on her street, like there was some sort of invisible string tugging me along. And I continued on, further up into the mountains where Pop's house was—where *our* house was.

Suddenly it wasn't just the emotions of seeing Amber after so long cascading through me, but a bundle of nerves at being inside this house again.

When I'd returned for his funeral a few months before, I had avoided the house. I hadn't admitted that to anybody, but I couldn't handle the thought of walking around that house without him. I stayed at a hotel a few miles from town to put as much distance between myself and Palmer as possible.

But now I think that was a mistake because maybe if I had been brave enough to walk into this house before now, it wouldn't be so damn hard. Even as I drove up the front drive, it seemed impossibly quiet.

I sat in the driver's seat and gripped the wheel, looking through the window for a long time, listening to the sounds of birds chirping in nearby trees.

Finally, when I couldn't stand the sound of my own breathing anymore, I climbed out of the truck, routing around in my pocket for the old familiar key that let me into my childhood home.

The familiar scent of my father assailed my nostrils—wood stain, cooked bacon, and his cologne. How did it still cling so heavily to the air after all this time? Maybe it was all in my head, I reasoned.

The place was neat as a pin, just like my father always kept it. He kept up with the mantra of his mother, "a place for everything and everything in its place." He was a particular stickler for that with his toolbox, and it was a tradition I proudly carried on.

The place still felt like home. There were large windows towards the front of the house where you could see the mountains and the sun poured in the mornings, just like now. It still took my breath away.

I ran my fingers over the carefully crafted cabinets that my father planed and stained himself.

I entered the kitchen and, as if on cue, my stomach started grumbling. I don't know why I opened the fridge expecting to find anything edible. The place had been unoccupied for three months. Anything left in here would be suspect.

I laughed at my stupidity, but that laugh died in my throat as soon as I saw what was decorating his fridge. There were a few thank you notes from clients, then mostly pictures of me at various ages, along with pictures of Amber and Abigail. There were a couple of drawn pictures, and I recognized Abigail's handiwork. It matched the side of that bakery box I'd pilfered three months before.

I'd known they were close, but seeing the evidence all over Pop's fridge made the look in Amber's eyes stab at me all the more sharply.

My eyes drifted to a picture of Amber with her arm around her little girl, who looked just like her. The warmth in those big brown eyes never left me and after our near collision in the grocery store, I easily fell into their velvety depths—that's what first attracted me to her.

I'd been making a grand fool of myself in the hallway between classes when I slipped and fell square on my ass. My buddies just laughed, but Amber rushed over and held out her hand to help me up. There was unyielding kindness in her eyes, and I was relieved to see it was still there, especially after I had let her down so many years ago.

I almost wished she would have looked at me with rage or cold indifference. It probably would have been a hell of a lot easier to deal with.

"Remember what you're here for Liam," I reminded myself out loud. Now that I was back inside the house, it was going to be even harder than I imagined clearing the place out to sell it. I'd grown up here—taking my first steps, breaking my first bone, having endless good times with Pop.

This is the house I'd snuck out of to meet Amber in the middle of the night. This was the place I'd brought her to meet Pop, and I still remembered the look of wonder on her face at our view of the mountains. That was the moment I knew I loved her. It took a special person to appreciate the quiet and peaceful life we enjoyed here.

Without realizing it, I had reached for the picture, rubbing my thumb over her sweet face. Once I realized what I was doing, I dropped it as if it had burned me, forcing myself to focus on what Pop left behind. There would be a lot of packing to do, and no doubt it would be tedious and difficult. I didn't think much repair would be required, because Pop was a meticulous carpenter, and he never let things go untended.

Just as I had that thought, I turned on the faucet to get a glass of water, and it sprayed everywhere—all over me, and most of the kitchen.

I quickly squatted beneath the sink to turn off the water. Once I cleared my eyes, I grabbed a nearby tea towel to soak up most of the mess. "Okay, pipes need a clear out. No big surprise, considering this place has been sitting stagnant for months," I mused, making a mental checklist of what needed to be worked on.

But I knew I could count on the rest of the house to be pretty sound. Those who spent time with Pop before he'd died said he'd been feeling good, so there'd be no reason for projects to remain unfinished.

Once again, I'd barely had the thought when a piece of molding over the cabinet fell off and clattered to the floor.

"What the hell?" I asked the kitchen, and that's when I heard it: quiet and insistent.

I moved towards the large window at the front of the house and sure enough, there were two doves roosting in the trees right outside the house.

"All right, old man, what are you up to?" I asked aloud. I would continue to ask that question as I methodically worked my way through the house and found a long list of items that needed to be fixed—simple stuff that Pop would've never left unfinished.

I knew he hadn't been feeling unwell in the months leading up to his death. He said he felt fine and the people of Palmer would have reached out if they thought something was wrong. From what I'd gathered at the funeral, everybody was as shocked as I was that he'd passed so suddenly. More than one person told me they thought he was "fit as a fiddle," and that they couldn't believe he was gone.

But I smelled something fishy. I didn't believe in otherworldly things, but if anyone could reach across from the dead to the living, it would be Pop.

I tapped against the note in my shirt pocket. "You trying to keep me here longer than I need to be, old man?" I asked to the ceiling.

In answer, a bird tapped on the window... and the old window splintered in response. "You have got to be kidding me!"

"All right, Pop, I hear you. Quit pushing," I smiled and shook my head.

I would do what needed to be done here, and it would take as long as it would take. Clearly all these minor repairs were Pop's way of telling me to get uncomfortable and face my fears, or more specifically, face Amber.

I ordered a pizza and sat watching videos on my phone to entertain myself, when the phone in my hand started buzzing. I answered and was surprised to hear a familiar voice.

"Liam, my man. A little birdie told me you were back in town," Tom Rockefeller said enthusiastically. Tom and I were buddies in high school, but we had lost touch and were mostly social media friends now. I knew he had gotten married and had two kids, but Tom started talking like we chatted every day.

He filled me in on what his kids were up to and that he and his wife were about to celebrate their tenth wedding anniversary.

"That's great man! Congratulations. Ten years is no small feat," I laughed. Not like I had any personal experience, but I would play along.

"Yeah, we've packed a lot into those ten years, so I want to make sure we do it right. We're going to be hosting a party in a few weeks to celebrate and if you're still here, we'd love for you to come."

"Well, I appreciate that, but I'm not sure I'll be here that long."

"I understand you have a life back in Austin. But I was thinking while you're here, I might throw a little work your way... I'm doing pretty well now, and I know every little bit helps."

I bit my lip. Nobody knew how well I was doing in Austin. Pop bragged about my carpentry skills and the satisfaction of my clients, but he didn't share the details of my financials. It just wasn't his style. And I typically wasn't candid, either. People treated you differently when they knew you had money, and sometimes it was difficult to tell if their interest was genuine.

"Oh yeah? What exactly did you have in mind?" I asked, out of curiosity.

"We're fixing up the entire house, but we're planning to have this party in the backyard. Sheila wants it to be perfect, of course—you know she's an interior designer, so everything has to be just so. But I'm thinking it would be nice to have a pergola... and don't tell anybody, but we're going to surprise the guests by renewing our vows."

"Wow, that's pretty cool," I said, not quite knowing what else to say. There was a time when I thought I'd be married to Amber with kids by now. But I'd let her mother's words occupy my head and mess that up for us, and now I was finding myself envious of Tom and his family.

I swallowed that back and congratulated him again as he gave me more details about the pergola he wanted.

By the time I got off the phone, I had directions to Tom's house, and a meeting set up for the next day to see the space. Tom had a pretty good idea of what he wanted, but he wanted my input on what would work best.

I'd been back in Palmer less than twenty-four hours and in that time I'd run into the love of my life, gotten several messages from Pop channeled through his deteriorating house, and booked a job with somebody I hadn't seen since high school. Little did Tom know I had no intention of taking his money. As excited as he sounded about the surprise for his wife, I would be more than happy to help him out.

Maybe it would help keep my mind off the more challenging parts of my to-do list... like making amends with Amber.

Amber

"Bye sweetie, have a good day at school," I called after Abigail. She waved her sweet little hands back at me, then skipped off through the doors with her friend.

I rushed back to the car and hurried back to the house to change out of my sweats and do something with my hair because I had a big meeting with a potential client this morning.

Sheila Rockefeller was quite the woman about town. In fact, she was quite a woman across several towns. I didn't know her all that well, but I remembered her husband Tom from high school. He met Sheila at the University of Colorado. She's the former Miss Pueblo County, and now is the hottest designer on this side of the Rockies. She's even been on one of those home makeover shows.

Apparently, she'd also been a guest at some parties where I'd provided the cake and got my information from one of my clients for which I was so grateful. I valued all my customers, but the recognition provided by doing a cake for someone like Sheila Rockefeller could jumpstart my business and bring me closer to finally opening my own store. It was so close I could almost taste it.

I needed to dress to impress for this meeting. I put on my makeup and I tried my hair in three different styles. Honestly, I hadn't messed with it this much since the last time I'd been on a date. Although, to be fair, it was a setup and one I hadn't been looking forward to. But to people like Sheila, appearance mattered, so I couldn't stroll in there with yoga pants and a messy bun.

I finally settled on brushing my hair down so that it fell in loose and wavy curls around my shoulders. I put on a flattering cream colored, silky button-down, and tucked it into an A-line skirt that fell just past my knees. It was casual, but still professional enough for the likes of Sheila—at least, I hoped.

I hurried out to my car and typed in the address to Sheila's house into my GPS. She and Tom lived on the outskirts of town, where the wealthier residents lived.

As I drove along, I mentally prepared my spiel for Sheila, but I kept getting distracted. Of course, that was non-stop since I literally almost ran smack-dab into Liam Murphy's crotch.

I couldn't take a breath without thinking about it. It was one thing to have that ghost haunting my thoughts, but it was quite another to know he was back in town... and he looked even better than he had the last time I had seen him.

It was unfair that the man who crushed my heart looked so damn good after all these years. It seemed only appropriate after that kind of heartbreak he should be missing teeth or balding. But alas, Liam Murphy looked like he just walked off the cover of a magazine—tall and rugged, but with classically handsome features. And I hated it, or more like I hated how much it made my heart race inside my chest.

Liam made a lot of girl's hearts race in high school, and I distinctly remember being flabbergasted that he wanted my attention.

Liam had always been quiet, surly even, but once I got to know him, I realized he was just shy.

I wasn't particularly boisterous or outgoing. Sandra Davis insisted I display manners at every opportunity. This was exactly the reason I'd waded in between the crush of laughing high school boys to help Liam up off the floor when he fell in the hallway. Or more likely, was pushed.

It was one of those cheesy movie moments where our hands touched and electricity pulsed up my arm. But what made it worse was it was obvious Liam was feeling it, too.

We stopped and stared at each other while those dumbass boys made smooching noises. Liam tersely reprimanded them, "Hey, she's helping unlike you a-holes."

"Get your head in the game, Amber. This meeting is too important to be derailed by him," I muttered to myself as I neared the Rockefeller estate.

Once upon a time, I lived in a house nearly this big, but it all went away when my ex-husband decided he was done with family life. Even though he came from money, his parents weren't interested in keeping his soon-to-be ex-wife and his daughter afloat. Abigail got birthday cards from her grandmother, but that was the only contact she had with his side of the family.

As much as it pained me, it was easier to keep things to our little family, and I dreaded the day when my ex might decide he wants to come back and be a part of his daughter's life. As much as I want her to have a father, he fucked things up so horribly that I didn't want to risk him hurting her again. The one thing I could be grateful for was she was young when he left, so she didn't remember him well. There wasn't much of him to miss.

It was a sad state of affairs, but I was busting my ass to make up for his absence and I had good people around me to help, too. Patrick had filled the male role model spot perfectly.

"Oh, Patrick," I sighed as I parked in front of the Rockefeller's place. "I really wish you were here."

The Rockefeller house was impressive, and once I was ushered inside by a housekeeper, I admired how immaculately decorated it was, but it also made me really grateful for my little house. It was warm, cozy, and cluttered, but it was full of love. I'm sure the Rockefellers had love too, but the house was almost austere in its decorations. It was perfect for a magazine, but not ideal for a family to roughhouse and live in.

"Amber," Sheila sang out to me as she strode towards me down a long hallway. "I hope you didn't have any trouble finding the place."

I shook my head. "Not at all. I grew up here, so I can find my way anywhere," I assured her.

She leaned in and gave me an air kiss on each cheek. "I can't thank you enough for taking the time to meet with me. I'm very excited to hear about this party you're throwing," I said in my most congenial, businesslike voice.

"Yes! There's so much to plan. You know we were just going to do a small family get-together, but that never lasts long with me and Tom, you know. Our guest list of sixty is now up to a hundred," she laughed as if this was an everyday problem.

My eyebrow shot up. "Wow, well then, you're going to need a good-sized cake. Tell me what you were thinking about for the desserts."

She put up a hand. "In good time. First, let me show you around the house so you can get a feel for the place and be inspired."

That statement made me a little nervous. In my bag was a notebook with laminated pictures of recipes and finished cakes I thought might interest somebody like Sheila. But it sounded like she had something completely different in mind.

I smiled and nodded as she showed me the rest of the home, which was immaculate. I peered over her shoulder, trying to find a toy stuffed under the bed at least. But from what I saw, nothing was out of place. It was a magazine spread all the way.

Privately, I thought Abigail would hate living like this. She loved spreading her little horse figurines out across the coffee table and playing make-believe, and I loved watching her from the kitchen as I worked. She was supposed to clean them up when she was done, but often it didn't happen. I probably should have scolded her for that, but something tugged at my heart when I strolled into the living room each morning and saw her horses scattered across the table—evidence of the happy, playful girl I was raising.

As we chatted, I interjected different ideas about various cakes. To my relief, Sheila was pretty receptive to all of my ideas. So, by the time we got to the back porch, we had narrowed it down to a couple of different selections.

That's when she swept out an expansive gesture towards the back door as if she was Vanna White.

"And this is where the party will take place. I've been working nonstop with the landscaper to find the right shrubs and flowers for the occasion. And Tom is out in the yard with one of his old contractor buddies coming up with some fresh addition to the yard that I'm pretty sure is supposed to be a surprise," she said conspiratorially. "Because he's being very hush-hush about it."

She opened the double doors with a flourish, and I stepped out onto the back deck. In the distance, I could see Tom talking to someone with a frame that was long and lean, and my heart nearly stopped.

It can't be...

Tom turned and waved to his wife, and she trotted down the stairs, beckoning me to come with her. I trailed behind her slowly as she called out to her husband,

"We don't mean to interrupt man-talk. I just wanted to introduce everybody."

"Well, there's no need for that. These two know each other *really* well, if you know what I mean," Tom said, waggling his eyebrows at his wife.

"Oh," she said with a smile.

I nearly choked on the breath I just took in. "That was in high school, a lifetime ago. We're not the same people anymore."

Liam hadn't said a word, but he kept his eyes on me the entire time, and it was torturous.

When he finally spoke, the timbre of his deep voice danced up my skin, causing goosebumps to breakout as he said, "Oh, I don't know Amber. I haven't changed that much. I still like the same things."

Tom snorted. "All I remember you being interested in high school was Amber."

Liam just looked at me and the attention made me blush.

A chirping sound interrupted our walk down memory lane, as Tom fished his phone out of his pocket, glancing at the screen and then looking at his wife with concern, "Sweetheart, it's the band again. Now they're saying they can't do it on the fifteenth."

"You have got to be kidding me? We've been through three bands already," she huffed before looking at Liam and me apologetically and saying, "I'm so sorry. Would you both excuse us? We should deal with this right away. You would not believe how difficult it is to hire a decent band around here," she said, as if this was something either of us dealt with regularly.

I nodded to her politely as she and Tom hurried back towards the porch, Sheila in his ear the entire way.

Reluctantly, I turned back to Liam, and we shared an awkward silence before he said, "Didn't imagine I'd see you here." And his rumbly voice undid yet another knot of irritation within me.

"Well, I certainly didn't think I would see you again so soon. Sheila's hiring me to make a cake."

"Good choice," he said simply.

"I didn't realize you and Tom were still for chummy."

This made him snort. "The last time I spoke to Tom in person was at high school graduation. He called me yesterday and said he had a project he needed help with for this big party they're having."

I nodded, "I see... well, I think all things considered we should steer clear of one another," I said, looking him in the eye, daring him to fight me.

I needed to take charge of this situation before it got out of control. This job was much too important to my family and my business to let anyone get in my way, especially Liam. I wouldn't let my high school sweetheart bring me down.

To my immense irritation, Liam laughed. "I hardly think I'd be in your way of making cakes."

I stiffened my shoulders and stuck my nose in the air. "You've been back in town for a day and you've already been in my way," I told him.

"Do you mean the grocery store?" He asked incredulously. "Well, excuse me for daring to shop at the grocery store. I didn't know you had claimed that turf. Do you want me to dine at the gas station for the rest of my time here?"

I glared at him. "You don't have to be so snippy about it."

"Apparently I do. I know I'm not your favorite person, but we're both adults. Is it necessary for us to avoid each other like we're in grade school and can't be trusted to sit next to one another? Do you hate me that much?" He said, his voice growing angry.

I don't know what possessed me. I should've stepped away, and yet I stepped closer to him, getting into his space. "What boggles my mind is you think it odd I wouldn't want to be around you. If you must know, this is a very important job for me and my business, and I cannot afford to be distracted."

"So I distract you, huh?" He said with a mischievous grin.

"What? That's not what I meant." I said, flustered.

"Then what exactly did you mean?" He said, stepping a little closer to me. All I could smell was his cologne. After all these years, he hadn't changed it—the same musky scent I used to revel in. I remembered winters back in high school when he would loan me his jacket. I would stick my nose in the collar, and inhale the scent of him—his smell is branded into my memory.

"You are still the most infuriating man I have ever met," I hissed, not able to stop the words rushing out of my mouth.

Liam cocked one eyebrow, a smile tugging at his lips—a reaction that only infuriated me more.

"I guess some things never change," his voice rumbled, his eyes darting to my mouth.

I felt my eyes widen. *What the hell was happening?*

"You know, you really have some nerve," I spat out.

He nodded. "Yeah, I guess I do."

The next thing I knew, Liam's hand was on my waist, pulling me to him. Then his lips were on mine. That sweet, musky smell of him was enveloping me and I inhaled deeply, losing myself in it, just as my body responded to the feel of his lips after so long. They were just as soft, yet so much more demanding.

Suddenly, I heard voices in the distance, and alarm bells started going off in my head. As Liam and I broke apart, I panicked. I glanced toward the porch where Tom and Sheila were heading back down the stairs. They were talking intensely to one another and didn't appear to have seen us in our embrace.

I sucked in a deep breath, my hand going to wipe my mouth as I put several steps between myself and Liam.

His cheeks were red, but his eyes never left mine as I smoothed my hands over my skirt, hoping nothing looked out of place.

"I am so sorry about that, you two," Sheila said.

"It's no problem," I said a little too brightly. "Can I take another look at your kitchen? I'd like to get an idea of the working space, and then we can discuss what samples you'd like to try before you make a final decision," I told Sheila, hoping my taking charge attitude didn't rub her the wrong way. I needed to get away from Liam as quickly as possible. It was just like high school. One minute we were arguing, and the next we were making out like our lives depended on it.

It would hardly do for my new client to catch me pinned to a tree by my high school sweetheart, racing toward a very long, awaited orgasm and not giving a shit who saw us.

That was the thing about Liam... my mom worked so hard to raise me to be a lady and have manners, but Liam made me throw all that out the window.

I blame young love. But now here I was in my early thirties, feeling the same pull to him.

I dared a glance over my shoulder as I stepped through the back door. Tom was talking animatedly with his hands, but Liam was watching me carefully, like a wolf on the hunt.

If he was going to be in town for an extended period of time, I was going to have to stay far away. I'd been worried about the pain and heartache of running into him, but now I had something more pressing to worry about—I still wanted him.

I spent the rest of the day trying my damnedest to focus on the task at hand... and failing miserably.

My brain kept replaying our kiss over and over, and I couldn't get his intoxicating scent out of my head. It was like he'd drugged me.

"Amber? Amber? Hello?" A voice called out to me. I shook myself free of my reverie and focused on the voice.

Lena Williams. Lena was in charge of the diner, which was a couple of doors down from the empty storefront I was so in love with. She was a transplant to Palmer, having arrived seven years earlier.

In fact, a part-time server gig at her diner was one of the myriad of jobs I had before I started baking full time. And Lena was always nice enough to offer me a shift whenever I needed it to fill in any financial holes. Thankfully, for the last year I hadn't needed to as my cake business had covered all our bills.

I would never forget Lena's kindness. After my ex left, Abigail and I would come in and she would always feed us on the house. And I was pretty sure she still put an employee discount on my orders, even though I was no longer an employee. She was the closest thing I had to a best friend around here. Somebody who didn't remember me from high school and didn't care that I hadn't turned out the way everyone expected me to.

"You okay, girl?" She asked, concerned.

I shook my head, "Yeah... yes, I'm fine. Just tired."

She snorted. "What else is new? There's something else going on here, though. This wouldn't have anything to do with that tall drink of water who blew into town yesterday, would it?"

I looked at her in mock outrage, "What on earth would give you that idea?"

She rolled her eyes. "You forget, I have the memory of an elephant. You mentioned an old high school sweetheart breaking your heart, and you even told me his name. I don't know any other Liam who grew up here and who also happens to be Patrick's son."

"You saw him?"

"Mm-hm, he came in for a takeout order earlier. I can see why you're all hot and bothered right now."

"I am hardly hot and bothered," I protested.

She laughed. "Please, you're practically melting."

I rolled my eyes. "I just have a lot going on right now. You know I'm doing that cake for the Rockefellers."

She nodded in understanding. "That's no small deal."

"No, it isn't. So the last thing I need is to deal with is... him," I nearly growled out.

She eyed me speculatively. "And exactly how are you having to deal with him? Is he bothering you?"

I shook my head. "Not in the way you're thinking. This is a small town. We're going to run into each other and we've already run into each other twice. The first time I made an utter fool out of myself. The second time we ended up kissing, and I felt out of control. It's all nonsense. I need to get a hold of myself and..."

"Hold up a minute, back up. Did you say you ended up kissing?" She asked, thoroughly riveted now.

I looked around, grateful it was the quiet time of day. There were a few of patrons at various tables having their coffee, looking at their newspapers, not the least bit interested in the juicy conversation going on at the counter.

I sighed, then regaled her with what happened. By the time I was done describing how everything went down, she picked up one of the menus so she could fan herself.

"Damn, sounds like old boy still has a thing for you."

"If he still had a thing for me, he wouldn't have avoided this town for so long, and he certainly wouldn't have left the way he did... not that it matters now. We're getting off track," I said, irritated.

"Okay, let's look at the situation. There's likely one of two things going on here. Either you still have feelings for your old boyfriend and that's something you need to explore. Or perhaps you just need to feel something, period—it has been a while, Amber."

I raised my eyebrow in question.

Lena quickly continued. "Think about it. That dumb-dumb you called a husband has been gone for five years. You have been working non-stop, and you were working non-stop before he was gone. You're still a young, desirable woman—you have needs. Not to over-step any boundaries, but Ethan didn't strike me as the kind of guy who knew how to get it done in the sack. Am I right?"

I blushed. My ex, Ethan, hadn't been all that thought-ful between the sheets. Before we got married, he tried harder, but it was never the level of passion I had with Liam. By the time I met him, I had resigned myself to the fact that lightning doesn't strike twice. I loved Ethan in my way, and it didn't matter to me we didn't have the same chemistry. As far as I was concerned, that kind of chemistry brought trouble.

Unfortunately, what little effort he put in before we were married evaporated into thin air after we got married, and more so after I had Abigail.

"The look on your face says it all," Lena laughed.

I sighed, "I don't know. The timing couldn't be worse."

Lena eyed me sympathetically. "Look, don't worry about the Rockefeller gig. You always knock it out of the park. As for Liam, you just have to trust yourself more. You're not that teenage girl anymore—you're a strong, resilient woman with a mind of her own. So if you decide to get yourself a little something-something with the old beau, who cares as long as you don't get hurt?"

I appreciated Lena's support, but that was the thing—I wasn't sure I wouldn't get hurt. Every time I thought of Liam, much less saw him, I felt like the walking heartache I had been all those years ago.

"Or, you can give yourself a little treat after this event is over by getting on one of those dating apps and arranging yourself a hookup to service your needs. No shame in that."

I laughed. I could never see myself doing that, but it was a nice reminder from my friend I wasn't a heartbroken girl anymore—I was a grown woman who has kept everything together during some really trying times, and I needed to trust my instincts more.

Lena and I caught up on all the other things before I said my goodbyes and headed home. I probably shouldn't have dillydallied so long at lunch, but it was a much-needed break with my friend. And I felt like I had some renewed energy when I walked into my kitchen that afternoon.

"Liam be damned. Let's get started," I told my kitchen, setting to work on making samples for Sheila and forging a positive path for my future.

By the time I brought Abigail home later that afternoon, I had my samples prepared for Sheila that I would drop-off the next morning. I thought I'd be working on them all night, which is why I'd arranged for Abigail to sleep over with her grandmother.

Now I wasn't sure what I would do with an entire evening to myself. I was tempted to ask Abigail if she wanted to stay home and we could build a fort in the living room, but she was so excited about the sleep-over with her grandma. They had already made all these plans, so I didn't have the heart to ask.

I made sure she had her overnight bag ready when Mom arrived.

"Oh, what is that delicious smell?" Mom cooed as she came in the house. She hadn't exactly been supportive of my business when I first started. She thought I should find something more stable. But she didn't understand I would have to work at least two, maybe even three jobs, to provide the stability she thought we needed—and I would hardly see Abigail. I took the risk on the baking business so I could work from home and see my kid. It had been a gamble, but I was desperate enough to try it, and so far it was paying off even if it was a lot of work and money was tight most of the time.

I knew she was waiting for the moment to tell me, "I told you so." Those seemed to be my mother's favorite words, after all. But she has slowly warmed up to the idea, asking more thoughtful questions about my projects and what I had planned for the future. When I told her I was going to do an event for the Rockefellers, her eyes lit up. "Oh, they have money. Amber, this could be a big deal for you."

She didn't have to tell me twice. It was only the refrain that ran through my head every other minute.

"Thanks, I really hope she likes them," I said as I double-checked Abigail's backpack to make sure she had everything she needed. "I really appreciate this, mom."

"Oh, it's no problem. I get to spend the evening with my beautiful granddaughter, and we are going to do a little makeover," she informed me.

Abigail was already jumping up and down.

"I even went to the drugstore this morning and got three new colors of nail polish for you to try, young lady," Mom told Abigail, to her delight.

"I want to try hot pink," Abigail informed her grandma, much to her dismay.

"Hot pink? What is this generation coming to?" She lamented, looking at me in question.

I bit back a laugh. Leave it to my mother to be scandalized by hot pink—surely not a "lady-like" color in her head. If I had to guess, she had three different shades of delicate pink in her bag from the drugstore that, from a distance, no one would ever be able to tell the difference between.

"All right, you two, don't party too hard," I said, winking at my daughter.

Abigail gave me a droll look. "Come on Mom, this is Grandma we're talking about."

Mom scoffed in mock outrage and I laughed, but Abigail had hit the nail on the head. If I knew my mother, they would enjoy pedicures, finger sandwiches, and maybe if she was feeling a little frisky, a little chocolate before bed, but otherwise, it would be a fairly sedate night for these two.

I waved them off and shut the door behind them, then took in the empty house.

It was funny, as a Mom I was always looking for a few precious minutes to myself, but the second Abigail was gone I missed her. And then I remembered I could take a long, hot shower without distraction.

Happily, I marched into my bedroom, turned on my favorite Pandora station and took some time to do the things I never had time for. With a little effort, I could look like the caliber of woman that Sheila Rockefeller was used to doing business with.

After I luxuriated in a long, hot shower and did my nails, I inspected myself in the mirror and gave myself an approving nod. "Not too bad for somebody who routinely works on four hours of sleep," I told my reflection, and then my thoughts drifted. "Liam didn't seem to mind... wonder what he would think now."

"Uh, it doesn't matter," I said succinctly. "Great, now I'm talking to myself. Enough of this nonsense. Time to relax."

I slipped into my favorite Foo Fighters t-shirt and pajama shorts and made my way back to the living room. I plopped myself down on the couch, turned on the TV, and started scrolling for a rom-com. Except my mind kept straying to the feel of his lips against mine. His kiss had been more intense, more desperate than it had been in high school. I wondered if he would bring that kind of enthusiasm to other interactions.

I groaned aloud to the empty room, frustrated that my brain could think of nothing else. Once I had forcefully reprimanded myself, yet again, to focus on the TV screen in front of me, the doorbell rang.

"Who in the world could that be at this time of night?" I muttered to myself as I heaved myself from the couch and strode to the door. I wasn't prepared for who I saw through the peephole.

I hesitated before I finally opened the door, feasting my eyes on the man who had been wreaking havoc on my mind—and body—for most of the evening. "Liam?"

He dressed down from when I saw him this morning, standing on my porch in a heather grey t-shirt that hugged his broad shoulders and snug blue jeans.

"Hey Amber, I'm sorry to drop by unannounced, but..." He rubbed an anxious hand over his face and finally met my eyes, "I need to talk to you. Do you think you could spare a few minutes?"

His request knocked the wind out of me, but I moved to the side as an invitation to come in without really thinking it through.

He ducked inside, his eyes taking in everything. My house was clean, but cluttered. It was nowhere near as pristine as Rockefellers. It was obvious a child lived here and I couldn't help but wonder what he thought as he took it in. This was my home, where my life happened, and for some strange reason I wanted to know what he thought of it when he saw it.

"I hope I'm not interrupting your routine," he said, looking back at me nervously.

I shook my head. "Normally yes. But Abigail's having a sleepover with my mom tonight."

He shook his head, and I couldn't help but notice the way his mouth tightened at the mention of my mom. It was a quick observation that I let go just as quickly.

"Oh, where are my manners? Please sit down. Would you like something to drink?"

"No, you don't have to do that, Amber. It's just me, I'm hardly company," he said, moving to stand in front of the couch, but not sitting down.

"Look, I've been needing to do something for a long time and I've been too chickenshit to do it. But since Pop's gone..." He stopped, shuddering briefly and looking down at his boots before finally looking up into my eyes. "Amber, I'm really sorry for how I ended things back in high school. I was young and stupid. I got these ideas in my head that I shouldn't have, and I know that's no excuse for my behavior. And I know I can't take it back, but I need you to know there's not a day that goes by that knowing I hurt you doesn't tear me up."

I stood, stunned, with my mouth hanging open. I had every intention of being gracious—that was the young lady my mom raised me to be—but that's not what came out of my mouth. "You could've fooled me," is what I said instead.

He looked like I'd just kicked him in the stomach.

"I mean, it's been thirteen years, Liam. If you felt so much remorse, what took you so long? What did you think was going to happen if you came apologizing now, exactly?"

He rubbed that nervous hand over his head again, ruffling his hair that was a need of a cut. "I don't know... and I can't blame you for feeling that way. I just felt in my gut it needed to be said. I thought for a long time it would be best to not say anything at all. But then Pop reminded me it's never too late..."

"Never too late?" I laughed glumly. "What the hell does that mean? Never too late for what?"

"I don't know Amber. It's just what he said. You know, Pop. He was always trying to fix things for people. I just figured it wasn't too late for an apology, for you to know I never meant..."

"No!" I said, putting up a hand to stop him. "No, this isn't the part where you tell me you never meant to hurt me because if you didn't, then you wouldn't have left... not that it matters now," I added, annoyed.

There was a wide swath of emotions playing over Liam's face, but in his eyes was the same determination

I had fallen in love with when we were kids. He wasn't going to let me get away with being sarcastic or catty, just like he hadn't back then.

He huffed out a soft laugh. "You could've fooled me," he said softly, throwing my words back in my face.

I shook my head at him, anger coursing through me. "Are you kidding me right now? You come in here with your apology and now you're taunting me?" I said, stepping closer to him. "You call that an apology?"

He shook his head, the corner of his mouth tugging up like it usually did when he was ready to fight. He closed the distance between us. "Don't go twisting my intentions here, Amber. I'm trying to apologize and you're telling me it doesn't matter. How can you say that after what happened this morning? I know you felt it. There's still something between us, you can't deny it."

"Is that why you're here, Liam? Trying to start up shit that's better left kicked over?"

His hand cupped my jaw then, his eyes alternating between my eyes and my mouth as he said in a low growl, "Maybe I am here to settle some unfinished business... although I'm beginning to think I'll never be finished with you, Amber," he said, and then his mouth was on mine again, and it was like no time had passed with the exception that this was more desperate, more urgent.

I don't remember the moment when I decided, but suddenly my fingers went to the hem of his t-shirt and yanked it up. It was a dance we hadn't done for thirteen years, but it felt like we'd been doing it every day without fail. The moves were muscle memory as he stripped off his shirt and slipped his hands beneath mine to palm my breasts, causing me to moan into his mouth.

My nipple beaded hard against his palm and I swallowed his growl as his tongue pushed between my lips and I finally got to taste him again. It was just like before, except richer and hotter. I clung to his shoulders, trying to pull him closer. I don't remember when my shirt came up over my head or when my shorts hit the floor, but the next thing I knew I was being laid back on my couch as a shirtless Liam loomed over me. He kneeled between my thighs, looking down at me like I had been the one to walk out on him and leave him high and dry. Like I was the one who needed to be reminded of everything that had been torn apart.

I couldn't handle the hurt in his eyes, so I reached for him, pulling him back down to kiss me and revel in the feel of his skin against mine.

His fingers were still tweaking my nipples as his mouth moved from mine, trailing kisses over my neck to that sensitive spot by my ear. I don't know why I was surprised he remembered the path and then his mouth was working its way over my chest, sucking one of those aching buds into his mouth. I arched off the sofa, moaning loudly into the still air. The only other noise in the house were sounds of some rom-com in the background.

I speared my fingers into his hair, holding his head as his hand skated down my waist, my thigh, and then my knee, positioning it so he could lean more comfortably in between my legs.

He released my nipple and kissed his way down my belly, past my belly button and the pregnancy stretch marks to the elastic band of my panties.

He looked at me, as if in question, and I nodded desperately. He hooked his fingers beneath the elastic, rolling the panties down my legs, and settled himself in between them, shoving his shoulders between my knees and spreading me wide for him.

He hovered over my crotch for a long moment, inhaling me. "God, you smell good. You're so beautiful, even more beautiful than I remember," he breathed, before dipping his head down and flicking his tongue against the aching bud at the crux of my thighs.

I cried out at his touch. It really had been too long, and it had been even longer since I felt this wanted—or this hot. It felt even more intense because he kept watching me as he nipped at my clit, licking and sucking it as his fingers found their way to my entrance, entering first one then two fingers inside, going gently at first and then pumping harder and faster as he licked me.

My hand clutched at his hair as the other clutched at the pillow behind my head, trying not to buck my hips up and take his head off. I cried out loudly into the still house, reveling in the sound of it along with his heavy breathing and the mumbled words he said in between sucking and kissing my pussy. "Fuck Amber. Oh, fuck, you taste so good. You have no idea how many nights I've dreamt about this... how bad I needed you... if all I ever get to do is taste you again, I'll die happy man."

His words made me clench hard around his fingers, and then I couldn't stop my hips from bucking up as my orgasm crashed through me, and I screamed out his name, "Liam!"

I rose beneath him, riding the waves of the most powerful orgasm I've had in years. Then he was holding me, cradling me to him.

Slowly, I opened my eyes and looked up at his lust filled gaze and I realized with startling clarity I hadn't even begun to feel sated.

I looked at him with determination. "Take off your pants," I instructed him.

He looked hesitant for a moment before his hands were fumbling with his belt. He shoved his jeans and underwear down, rising to his feet to take all of it down along with his boots, and tossed them aside.

And then my eyes feasted on the body I had dreamt about for far too long. However, this was no longer the body of a nineteen-year-old boy. There were scars and more muscles, but it was still just... him.

A warm sense of coming home was flooding through me, mixed with fresh new excitement as I reached for him, and we collapsed into one another's arms like a magnet was drawing us together.

That urgent embrace was familiar, but the feel of his hard, rugged muscles beneath my exploring fingers was new, and I reveled in the sensation they made as I ran my fingers down his arms, his back, over his buttocks and around his front to wrap around his hardness.

He moaned into my neck, and I felt an enormous surge of feminine power. I could get drunk off of that feeling.

"Amber," he whispered. "Please, I need to be inside you."

His plea was so raw and open, there was no way I could look into his face and see that same hardened expression he had given me all those years ago before he turned his back on me. No, this was a man who had been hurting for a long time, who had put this hard shell of a person over my Liam.

For a moment, I wanted to back away and examine him. To understand the pain in his eyes.

But my body had other ideas. I couldn't back away from him. Instead, I spread myself open for him and he looked into my eyes as if to be sure the invitation I was offering him was real. Once he saw I was serious, he poised himself at my entrance, still slick with the pleasure he had wrought from my body just minutes before. Then he slid inside of me and the feeling of emptiness I had been trying to ignore evaporated. Now that he was back, I wouldn't be able to let him go anytime soon.

He hesitated to give me time to adjust to him, but I wasn't having it. "No, Liam. Don't wait, give me what I need," I said.

He groaned at my entreaty and began moving his hips, slowly at first, but when my hands started clutching his shoulders, he picked up speed, filling me again and again, making sparks of pleasure shoot through my body. I was consumed by him. All I could feel, see, touch, and taste was Liam, and I did so ravenously as I kissed him, my tongue mimicking what our bodies were doing to one another.

"Amber," he moaned. "My sweet Amber," he said into my ear as his fingers dug into my hip. I could feel him getting tense, so I knew he was close, as the walls of my pussy spasmed tightly around him. "Liam," I moaned out. "I'm going to come again."

"I'm right there with you, baby. Come with me," he said breathlessly into my ear.

His words unlocked whatever control I had left in me and my second orgasm of the night raced through me. I looked up to see Liam watching me intently as his own orgasm stole over his body, and he tensed inside me, letting out a long, savage growl, "Fuck."

He collapsed on top of me, breathing raggedly into my ear and telling me, "Amber, that was so good... you are so good."

And I knew instinctively he wasn't referring to what we had just done. There was a revelation in his voice.

We lay in each other's arms for a long time, waiting for our pulses to calm. When he finally pulled back to look into my eyes, I was not ready to face an awkward conversation or the reality of the situation. I had been consumed by the reality of our situation for far too long. No, I wanted to stay in this moment of fantasy for a little while longer. So when he opened his mouth to speak, I put up my hand to cover it and shook my head, telling him softly, "Less talking. More kissing."

When I removed my hand, he was grinning at me.

He nodded and leaned down, proceeding to kiss me long and languidly. This would lead to our next bout of lovemaking, and mercifully, we fell asleep before either of us could ruin the moment with questions about how this night would change things.

As I drifted off to sleep in his arms, I pushed away the knot of worries. I would deal with the havoc this was sure to wreak in the morning. But for now, I just wanted to revel in the pleasure of being in Liam Murphy's arms once again.

LIAM

I never thought I would hold Amber in my arms again. And as sweet as those memories had been from our youth, the memories we made tonight were unbelievable. Both of us had grown and changed since we were younger, and this version of Amber deeply intrigued me. She was passionate and bold, not afraid to say what she wanted or needed. And I was so happy to deliver on both.

As I lay there listening to her soft breathing as she slept, everything just felt... right. For the first time in an impossibly long time.

I dozed off and slept peacefully for a time and then jerked awake every so often just to watch her again and take in this moment. I didn't know what was waiting for us on the other side of that sunrise, but I was going to soak up every bit of joy I could in this moment.

When the sun finally did rise, I heard the soft coos of doves just outside Amber's bedroom window and I had to smile.

Okay Pop, I hear you.

I nodded off again with my face buried in the sweet smell of her hair and dreamt of days spent with Amber—the smell of cake, and a plethora of portraits drawn by Abigail scattered all over the walls. It was a sweet place my brain visited—one without regrets and heartache.

As the sun rose higher and spilled through the curtains of Amber's bedroom window, she stirred and I woke with her, smiling down into her sleepy face.

She moaned into my neck, "Good morning."

"Yes, it is," I confirmed happily.

I could feel her smile curve against the skin of my neck when a creaking noise startled us out of bed.

"What is it? What's wrong?"

Before she could answer, I heard a voice calling, "Yoo-hoo, Amber? I brought your baby girl home."

Sandra.

The last time I heard that voice, it told me I would never be good enough for Amber and I would ruin her life if I tried to make it work. She demanded I leave town before I screwed up everything, and my dumbass had listened.

I hadn't heard her voice in thirteen years, and every detail of our interaction rushed back to me at the sound of it.

Amber hadn't noticed my concern because she was too busy frantically looking around. "We've gotta get you out of here," she whispered.

My brow furrowed. "Can I sneak out back?" I asked, already knowing the answer.

She plopped back down on the bed. "This is such a mess. I don't know how to explain this to Abigail, she's too young. You need to get dressed. Maybe we can say you were just visiting early."

She jumped out of bed quickly, tearing through her chest of drawers to put on some clothes and hollered at the top of her lungs, "I'll be right out, Mom! Slept through my alarm!"

"Shit, shit, shit," she muttered as she struggled to get her clothes on.

"Amber? Amber, come on, slow down. Remember, slow is smooth and smooth is fast."

She shot me a withering look. "Said by somebody who's never had a kid."

I shrugged. She wasn't wrong. "Quit lying there, staring at me, and get your clothes on," she said in a hushed voice as she covered her naked beauty, much to my despair.

"Oh, right. Sorry," I said, as I leapt out of bed to find my clothes.

"Mommy?" a little voice called out, and that's when it hit me how real this situation was. This was not how I wanted to meet Abigail, and this definitely wasn't how I wanted to face Sandra again after all these years.

"Coming, sweetheart," Amber called, looking over her shoulder at me one last time and urging me to "hurry" before rushing out the door.

I wasn't sure how I was going to manage this. Amber's bedroom was at the end of a long hallway, and the bathroom was right across from it. The door next to it,

I assumed, was Abigail's. Once I was dressed, I waited a few minutes, listening to their muffled voices down the hall as I assessed the situation. Amber's was more high-strung than usual.

I waited, and I waited, but I knew if I didn't act soon, I would be stuck. "Right, just act like you belong here," I said to myself as a reminder of something Pop often told me. If ever I was walking into a situation where I felt like I wasn't enough, he told me to go in with my head held high. This was no different... there was a hell of a lot more at stake, but I couldn't think about that right now.

Sucking in a deep breath, I opened the door and strolled down the hallway, closer to the voices. When I peered into the room at the mouth of the hallway, three heads looked at me simultaneously, all in surprise. Abigail's expression was curious, but Sandra's was pure shock. Amber just looked like she wanted to disappear.

"Good morning, ladies," I said jovially.

"Who are you?" Abigail asked curiously.

"This is an old friend of mine, Abby. This is Mr. Liam."

"Hi, Mr. Liam. How do you do?" She asked.

"I'm just fine, thank you very much," I replied, marveling at how much she looked like her mother. She even had the same curls spilling down her back. I knew very little about Abigail's father, but what I heard wasn't good. I was relieved to see she took mostly after her mom.

"Liam needed to use the restroom, so he stopped by because it was on his way."

"Oh, did you have a tummy ache?" Abigail asked.

"Abigail Grace..." Amber said in warning.

"What? You're the one who told me I can usually hold my tinkle, but tummy aches are a whole other story."

I laughed. "Well, you're right Abigail. I guess the coffee got to me this morning," I told her, making a face.

Abigail nodded solemnly, as if she understood this problem all too well. "My uncle Patrick used to tell me coffee was the elixir of the gods."

"Yes," I chuckled. "I remember him saying that."

"But he said it also gave him the trots," she said.

"Abigail," Sandra broke in.

I laughed even harder. "He said that too, and it did, as I remember."

"Do you know Uncle Patrick?" She asked with wide eyes.

There was a brief strained silence when Amber said, "Abigail, honey, this is Uncle Patrick's son."

Abigail looked surprised and delighted. "That's so cool you actually had him for a dad. Are you here to take his place?" She asked in all seriousness.

"Uh, not exactly. Nobody could ever take my dad's place. I'm sure you know that."

"You look like him," she announced. "Just not as wrinkly."

"Thanks, I will take that as a compliment."

She looked at me, raising a dubious eyebrow as if she couldn't understand how I could take it in any other way.

"So, that's your truck outside?"

"Yup, that's my truck."

"Do you build stuff like Uncle Patrick?"

"I do. In fact, that's my job. He taught me everything I know."

"Abigail sweetheart, I'm sure Liam has places he needs to be," Sandra said, looking at me warily.

I was more than a little satisfied knowing I spent the night with her daughter. I typically wasn't one for petty revenge, but considering what this woman did to blow up my relationship with Amber, I enjoyed answering Abigail while I looked at Sandra. "Oh, no, you ask all the questions you want, Abigail. It's way more interesting talking to you."

"Would you know how to build a bookcase?" Abigail asked earnestly.

"I would, I reckon I can build you just about any kind of bookshelf you'd like. "

"Good, because I really need one and so does mama for all her cookbooks," she said.

"Abigail, Liam is a busy man. I'm sure he doesn't have time to mess with bookcases and we're doing just fine without them."

"Actually, I would be more than happy to build a bookcase for you and Miss Abigail here," I said, ignoring Amber's warning look and Sandra's look of dismay.

"Can I help?" Abigail asked.

I looked at Amber, who blinked at me with pleading eyes, bewildered by her daughter's enthusiasm.

"That would be fun, Abigail. I think my dad would be proud of us tackling this project together," I told her, and I meant it. I could practically feel him beaming at the thought of me teaching this little girl how to make something with her own two hands, and that it was Amber's little girl made it all the better.

I didn't know exactly what I was trying to do here, and I got caught up in the moment, but it felt like the right thing to do.

"Um, that's very generous of you, Liam," Amber said stiffly. "What do you say, Abigail?"

"Thank you," she said with a bright smile.

"You're very welcome. Now we'll just have to figure out a time to work on this bookcase."

"Yes, we will," Amber interjected, "but now Liam has to go, so say goodbye."

"Bye Mr. Liam," Abigail said, waving, "it was nice meeting you."

"Bye Abigail, the pleasure was all mine. You have very nice manners."

"My mama taught me," she said.

"That doesn't surprise me at all," I told her, waving as Amber nearly shoved me out the door.

"Goodbye, Sandra," I called over my shoulder in a slightly less friendly voice.

"Liam," she ground out the syllables and I bit back a laugh. It was obvious time had not softened her, and I was still one of her least favorite people.

Even as she shoved me out the door, I enjoyed the feel of Amber's hand on my back as Sandra watched the whole thing.

Amber followed me out onto the front porch and quietly shut the door behind her before she lit into me and hissed, "What the hell do you think you're doing?"

"What?" I asked innocently.

She glared at me. "Look, last night was fun..."

"It was a little more than just fun, don't you think?" I asked her.

I knew I was right when she blushed, but she shook her head. "That's not the point. The point is, it can't happen again. So don't feel obligated to hang around here. You certainly don't need to promise my daughter you're going to do these things with her."

"Look, Amber, I know you're still pissed about what happened but..."

"But nothing. We're not kids anymore, Liam. I have a daughter to raise and she's counting on me, which means I need to stay focused. I can't afford to be dis-tracted by someone who only going to be here for a short time. It's not only my heart I have to look after now."

I nodded reluctantly. I knew I would die before I hurt her again, but I couldn't be too upset with her for feeling the way she did, and after everything she went through with her ex-husband, I couldn't blame her for being pro-tective of her daughter. She's being a good mom.

"If that's how you feel, I'll respect your wishes. But I'd still like to teach Abigail how to build a bookcase."

Amber looked at me for a long moment, and suddenly I could see just how tired she was. Not just because we'd been up for a good portion of the night, but how exhausted she was from life. I couldn't imagine what her life must have been like all these years, and suddenly I was even more angry with Sandra for chasing me away.

I never would have deserted Amber like her ex-husband did, and I definitely wouldn't have abandoned a little girl like Abigail.

It was that thought that made me more determined to see this bookcase project through.

"I know your heart is in the right place, but I don't appreciate you making promises to my little girl you're probably not going to keep."

"You make me sound like such a monster. Do you really think I'd break my promise to her?"

She stopped and looked at me pointedly. "You broke your promise to me."

Ouch.

I scrubbed a frustrated hand over my face. "I can't blame you for thinking that, Amber, but you're wrong. And I'm going to prove it to you. I'm going to be here for a while," I vowed, hearing how wishy-washy it sounded, but I couldn't promise to stay forever. I had a life in Austin, with a business and employees counting on me.

"Mm-hmm," she said, "I guess we'll see about that."

"We will," I said defensively. "And I will teach Abigail how to build a bookcase... it's what Pop would have wanted."

That made her stop cold.

She eyed me with a narrowed gaze. "Fine, but I set the schedule. And I swear to you, Liam Murphy, if you disappoint my little girl, it's not some heartbroken teenage girl you're going to have to deal with—it's going to be one pissed off mama. You got me?"

I saluted her and breathed out, "Yes, ma'am."

With that, she turned on her heel, marched into her house, and slammed the door behind her.

I let out a sigh and then bit back a chuckle. I hadn't argued with Amber in so long... and I felt alive, for what feels like the first time since I'd left Palmer thirteen years ago.

"Holy shit," I muttered to myself as I made my way down her porch steps into my truck.

I had come to this house the night before with the intention of apologizing and making amends with Amber. And I ended up in her arms, then her bed, and inside her. I had taken a simple act of contrition and made it unbelievably complicated. And yet, as I revved up my engine, I couldn't help but look back at the front door that just slammed in my face and smile.

Amber may not believe I can keep my promises, but I was going to prove to her I wasn't the same young man who ran away from her.

Amber

I avoided my mother's eyes as I peeked out the side-light window next to the front door to see Liam was still sitting in his truck. What the hell was he doing out there?

I needed him to leave and take all of his sexy mur-murings and confusing feelings and get as far away from here as possible. If I could punch a ticket for him to go straight back to Austin right then, I would. Even though the thought of him leaving again tore at my heart, which just infuriated me even more.

"You can't go down this road again, Amber," I whispered to myself.

"What was that, dear?" My mom called from behind me in the kitchen.

"Nothing Mom, just remembered something I need to add to the grocery list," I said idly as I peeked out the window again to see Liam's truck was finally gone. I should be relieved, but I felt a little knot of sadness to see the space empty now.

When I walked back into the living room, Abigail had plopped herself on the couch and flipped on the TV to watch Saturday morning cartoons. She'd pulled out her box of toys and was setting up a new horse stable with a furrowed brow of concentration.

When she noticed me, she smiled, "I like Mr. Liam, he's nice. And I can't wait for my new bookcase."

"Oh, sweetheart," I started and stopped myself. I didn't want to break her heart already. Maybe Liam would keep his word. "Listen, Mr. Liam is really busy, so it might be a while before he can work on your bookcase."

"That's okay. I am very patient," she informed me.

"Is that right?" I asked her. "You're not that patient when it's time for the cakes to come out of the oven," I reminded her with a smile.

She rolled her eyes at me. "That's different. Cake time is an eternity," she informed me.

I laughed and then made my way to the kitchen to face my mom.

She was busy scrubbing an already clean sink.

"Mom, what are you doing?"

"I know you have some more baking to do, so I thought I would help you clean up."

I looked at the sparkling sink and then I looked at her, not saying a word. This was her way of coping when she was upset. Maybe if she scrubbed that sink hard enough, she wouldn't feel it necessary to say anything about Liam.

I took some steps toward the pantry and started pulling out the ingredients I needed for this morning's baking job.

"I just think," my mom started, turning towards me with one hand on her hip and the wet sponge clutched in the other with a death grip.

Oh boy, here we go.

I turned to her, trying to look as sincere as possible. "Mom, it's not that I don't want to hear what you think. But it's not like you're going to say anything I haven't heard before. And he was here using the restroom, that's all."

Her lips pursed into a tight little bow. "Amber Davis, I am your mother, and I don't appreciate you lying to my face."

The sound of her frosty tone had me standing up, rod straight. And suddenly I felt like I was a kid again, being chastised. It took me a moment to remember I was in my own damn kitchen, in my own damn house.

"Mom, I understand you're worried, but there's nothing to worry about. I can catch up with an old... friend," I stuttered out.

"Ha!" she answered dramatically. "You two were never friends, you were always googly-eyed over each other, but he was never right for you, and that has not changed."

I felt my hackles going up. "Mom, to be fair, it's not like you know the man. And I'm not suggesting he is right for me—I'm saying there's no point in this conversation. I'm not interested in any man being the right man at the moment."

She pressed her lips together again and then said, "Well, I think that's very wise. You know you have so much going on..."

I had to laugh. "Please, you don't have to tell me." Then I softened my stance and leveled a calming gaze towards my mom. "Mom, I have my priorities straight, and nothing will screw that up."

Her stance relaxed, and she sighed. "I know, but you never quit worrying about your kids, no matter how old they are. You'll find out soon enough, my dear."

I shook my head. "Oh, I have no doubt. I'm sure I'll be worrying about Abigail until we're both old and gray. But at some point, you have to trust you raised me well enough to handle things myself."

"Easier said than done, although I tried."

"You did a great job, Mom, no complaints here," I said, closing the distance between us and giving her a hug.

She patted my back. "I just want you to be careful. Men like Liam make promises so easily, and then..."

I felt myself stiffen. "I know, Mom... you don't have to remind me," I said, turning back to the stove.

There was a strained silence before she finally said, "Well, I guess I'll let you and Abigail get on with your day."

I thanked her again for watching Abigail and gave her another hug before seeing her off.

When I came back in the house, I looked at my sweet little girl playing and then moved into the kitchen where my ingredients were waiting.

I had plenty to do, and I definitely didn't have the time or space to pine over Liam Murphy.

What happened last night would have to stay in the past, just like everything else about him.

The next couple of weeks would prove to be... challenging.

Liam was on my mind more than ever, and it wasn't just the memory of his sweet kisses or the way he played my body like an instrument that was haunting me. It was that he seemed to be—everywhere.

I couldn't go to the grocery store without running into him. When I went to look at my beloved storefront, he'd be across the street at the café. I knew he wasn't following me; it was just the nature of being in Palmer. Everybody saw one another pretty regularly, but it never mattered to me before now.

It wouldn't be such a big deal if it wasn't for the fact that every time I saw him, my heart would jump out of my chest like an overjoyed teenage girl. By the time my head hit the pillow every night, I'd expected to pass out exhausted, but no, I tossed and turned, remembering what we had done in this bed. I had been living off the memories of our stolen nights together when we were kids, but now I had a new one burning me up and it was driving me insane.

All things considered, I thought I put on a good face for Abigail and my mom. I still had our normal routine to maintain. Plus, I was hard at work preparing for the Rockefellers' party, which was in a couple of days. This was a monumental moment for my business, so I couldn't afford to mess up.

I was making one of those panicked grocery runs when I bumped into Liam. Again.

"We have to quit meeting like this," he said with a playful smile.

"For a man who lives on his own and is notably not a Top Chef, you sure are here an awful lot."

He shrugged his shoulders. "A man's got to eat. And as good as the food is at the diner, I don't feel like eating out every night."

"Have you grown antisocial in your old age, Liam?" I teased him.

He laughed. "I don't know, maybe. To be honest, I forgot how nice it is to be inside Pop's house. When you have that view to enjoy every evening, you don't want to be anywhere else."

"Well, I can't disagree with you there. It is a delightful house. It's going to be weird to think of somebody else enjoying it."

He sighed. "Yeah, it really is. I still have a lot to repair first."

My brow furrowed. I wondered why he had stuck around for so long. It was odd Patrick would have left unfinished projects—the house appeared well main-tained the last time I was there. "I was wondering about that. He took care of everything so meticulously."

He looked as confused as I felt. "Yeah, that's what I thought. But repairs keep popping up. If it's not a burst pipe, it's molding coming off the walls. If I didn't know better, I'd say his ghost is hanging around to mess with me," he laughed, and then we looked at each other for a long moment.

I shook my head. "No, that's ridiculous."

"Yeah," he agreed, although he didn't sound so sure.

"He was a crafty old bugger."

"Now that I cannot deny," he said with a wide smile. "Listen, I know you've been busy with the Rockefeller party coming up, but I was thinking once that's over I could work on the bookcase with Abigail?"

Panic rose inside me. "Oh... I don't know what our schedules are going to look like just yet."

"No, of course not," he said, "but I don't want to disappoint your little girl. She seems really sweet."

That made me feel guilty. I was pushing Liam away to protect myself, but if he was willing to do this for Abigail—and she was so excited about it—who was I to stand in the way?

I relented and said, "Let's get through the party first and then we'll set up a date, okay? Assuming you're still in town."

He gave me a wide, wicked grin. "Oh, I'm not going anywhere for a while..."

Dread and excitement bloomed in my guts, causing the most confusing of feelings.

My feelings must have played all over my face because he laughed, "Don't act too excited Amber. Like I said, there's a lot more to fix at Pop's house than I expected. Quality craftsmanship doesn't happen overnight, so you'll have to get used to running into me in the grocery store for a little while longer."

I glared at him. "It's a public space. Do what you want," I said, turning back to my cart and moving away.

That ornery grin stayed in place as he watched my every move. "See you later, Amber," he crooned.

"Right," I muttered, as I walked away.

Why did it feel like I had just run a marathon every time I spoke to that man? I was struggling for breath in the most undignified ways as I pushed my cart to the checkout line. The cashier was going to think I was hyperventilating.

I needed to get my shit together and figure out how I was going to coexist with Liam in this tiny little town without arguing with him or jumping his bones because, honestly, both were likely to happen.

"Keep your eye on the prize, Amber," I muttered to myself after I put my groceries in the trunk and settled back in the car.

It was the night of the Rockefeller party, and to say there were butterflies in my stomach was an understatement. It was more like a bear with sharp clawed nerves instead of gentle butterfly wings.

All the desserts were ready and packed. I just needed to load them into my car after my mom came to pick up

Abigail. I didn't know how long the party would last and I didn't want her waiting up for me. So, once again, Mom had volunteered for an impromptu sleepover.

"Mom, Grandma is at the door!" Abigail called from the living room. I was still in the bathroom, fussing with my makeup.

"Let her in, sweetie," I called out to her.

I could hear my mom's voice from down the hall as I put on the finishing touches and examined myself one last time in the mirror on my closet door.

Sheila wanted me to look like I was a guest, but I also needed to look professional, so I settled on a deep jade wrap dress that hit mid-calf and clung to all the right places without being too sexy. I'd worked my hair back into a French braid—nobody wanted to see the person serving food with their hair flying everywhere. And since it'd been cloudy and humid all day, I knew if I didn't put my hair back in a braid, the second I walked out the door, it would turn into a frizzy mess.

I strolled down the hallway to see my mother smiling and my daughter's face lit up.

"You look pretty, mama," she said. It was enough to make me want to burst into tears—the little things she said kept me going.

"Thank you, sweetheart," I said, kneeling down to hug her.

"You really do, honey," my mom said, holding back a smile.

I cocked an eyebrow. "What?"

She shook her head. "I'm just so excited for you. This is going to open up so many doors."

I let out a long breath. "I hope so."

"Remember, confidence!" My mother reminded me. "You walk amongst those richie-rich people like you are their equal—because you are, my dear," she coached.

I nodded in agreement. "Yes, I am," I said, looking down at Abigail with a wink.

As hard as life has been since her dad left, it was good for her to see her mom work hard and learn that no matter what, we would figure out a way through it. I wanted my daughter to be resilient and capable of handling herself out in the world—she came from a long line of strong woman. It was moments like these that gave me hope I would achieve just that.

"Oh, and don't forget your umbrella. I know the forecast says it's not supposed to rain, but it's getting darker out there," my mom reminded me.

"I've already got one in the car. I am just hoping to God the weather holds for this party."

"You and me both, sweetheart," my mom said. "Come on Abigail, let's go start our sleepover. Don't forget to wish Mom good luck."

"Good luck, Mommy. You'll do great!" She said, smiling up at me and I leaned down and gave her a bear hug.

I told them I loved them, to be careful and that I would call as soon as the party was over.

Once they cleared the driveway, I went about loading up the car, treading carefully so I wouldn't stain my dress.

As I drove out to the Rockefeller estate, I eyed the sky warily. Sunset wouldn't be for another couple of hours, but it didn't look like that at the moment. I wondered what kind of contingency plan Sheila and Tom had for bad weather.

As I pulled up to the house, I noticed a few cars were already there, presumably from the wait staff, as well as Liam's truck. It's as if just the thought of him made him materialize right before my eyes—and the next thing I knew he was opening my car door for me.

He gave a long, low wolf whistle when I straightened in front of him. "Really, Liam?"

"What? You look good. I didn't think the caterer was supposed to look better than the hostess," he said teasingly, and I rolled my eyes at him.

"What are you doing here?"

"Don't you remember? I am an invited guest. I mean, I built that damn pergola for Tom... oh, excuse me, we built it "together". That's what I'm supposed to tell everybody," he said conspiratorially.

"No, I mean, what are you doing out here with me?"

"Oh, I figured you would need some help getting your desserts inside."

He was genuinely offering me help, and I had to bite my tongue to stop from telling him I absolutely did not need it. I eyed all those large boxes in the back of my car—I really could use the help.

"Okay, but be super careful."

"Scouts honor," he said, "just tell me where I need to take them and what to do with them." I started giving him instructions, and we managed to move everything inside the house relatively quickly.

We were supposed to have the food set up outside on the porch, but considering the worrisome clouds hanging overhead, Sheila had the tables set up inside.

As we arranged things, I spied the new pergola outside.

"Wow, it's impressive," I said before I could stop myself.

I looked over at Liam, who was beaming proudly. "Thanks. Pop taught me a thing or two."

I nodded my head. "Well, thank you for your help. I've got it from here. Go enjoy the party."

Liam made a face. "Yeah, it's not really my scene. I was hoping I could help you out."

"Liam, why did you even come? I'm sure Tom would've understood."

He looked at me tenderly, then admitted, "Well, I thought maybe..." he paused, as if thinking better of whatever he wanted to say, then continued, "I thought maybe you could use some help."

I fought the urge to ask him what he really meant to say. "Well, I appreciate that, but I'm used to doing everything on my own."

"You're totally capable, Amber, but you don't have to do everything on your own," he said solemnly.

I could feel myself redden and an ache in my chest I'd been trying to ignore since we'd slept together sharpened. I swallowed hard around the lump in my throat. "Liam," I started.

"Amber, listen, that night..."

"Is not something I'm willing to talk about right now. I'm sorry, Liam, but this is a huge night for me and I can't afford for it to go sideways. So please, please can we stick a pin in it so I can make sure this evening goes off without a hitch."

He must've sensed my desperation because he nodded then, "Yeah, yeah... we'll talk later. It's going to go great for you, don't worry."

"There you are," Tom's voice called. "Liam, buddy, I want you to talk to this investor I play golf with. I think he would have some work to throw your way."

An odd expression crossed Liam's face. "Oh, goody," he said, exasperated.

"Hey the man is offering you work. You and I are not the type of people who can afford to turn that down," I lectured him.

He smiled tightly, "Yeah... sure. Look, I'll be around if you want to talk later tonight, okay?" He said, backing away towards Tom and his friends.

I nodded at him and then forced my attention back to setting up the food.

The party was... well, it was boring as hell. The guests seemed to talk about nothing but golf or their glamorous vacation homes. Thankfully, I got nothing but compliments on the desserts. Now I was just waiting for the big moment when Tom and Sheila would cut the cake. For all the class and finery of the party, they had chosen an unexpected cake design to celebrate their anniversary—a ball and chain.

The cake was out of place amongst all the pearls and designer shoes, but they were thrilled with the finished result.

Sheila encouraged me to mingle, but it was a little difficult to find things to talk about other than cake, of course. She introduced me to several women who were having parties in the coming weeks, and I was handed business card after business card, where I took notes on the type of party and any initial ideas they had. I promised everyone I would email them the following week to set-up tastings. I had to fight back my grin—it was happening. It was really happening, and I was so excited I could just dance.

In fact, this was the perfect time to dance, because the smell of rain was in the air. Liam and I always used to dance like fools in the rain, and that made me stop short.

Ever since he came back to town, memories of him hit me at the most inopportune times, but I couldn't seem to stop myself. I looked out across the groups of people on the back lawn, and my eyes caught his. He was standing by himself a fair distance away from the pergola next to a large oak tree, drink in hand, and he was watching me like he had been all night.

"This is ridiculous," I muttered to myself. The party was winding down as guests were leaving to beat the rain. It was time to get this dreaded conversation over with.

I worked my way through the crowd until I was face-to-face with Liam. He didn't smile when he saw me, but looked down at me intensely.

"Why do you look like you're about to beat my ass?" He asked me in a low, rumbly voice.

I pursed my lips together. "I would never do that."

He snickered, "At least not in front of all these people."

I rolled my eyes. "You wanted to talk. Let's talk."

He smiled then, but it didn't quite reach his eyes. "Oh, how romantic."

I sighed. "That's the point, Liam. We don't need to talk about romance. That night was a mistake, and I think you know that."

"No, I don't," he said insistently. "That is the last thing I would call it."

"Fine, then call it closure. Call it whatever you want, but it can't happen again."

"Why not?"

Those two words brought me back. They were so direct and were not anything I wanted to hear. "Liam," I nearly moaned.

"Don't tell me the night we shared meant nothing and then say my name like that. You're sending mixed signals, Amber."

"You are so insufferable," I hissed out, shaking my head.

He laughed, "You've said worse about me. I'll take it."

I looked at him and got incensed. "What do you want for me? You're acting like we can just pick up where we left off. But you seem to forget where we left off was you leaving me."

"I know Amber, and I can't seem to find the words to convince you that leaving you was the biggest mistake I've ever made."

"Really? Then why the hell did you? You keep acting like it's this big mysterious thing—like it's more complicated than I could ever understand. But it's not Liam, it's all too simple. You promised me forever, and then you broke that promise... and you broke me when you left," I ended quietly, fighting back tears that were threatening to spill down my cheeks.

He stepped closer to me, breathing out my name. "Amber," his hand was reaching for me.

"No! No, you don't get to come back here and sweep me off my feet and act like that didn't happen. I can't pretend like it didn't happen."

"I'm not asking you to forget Amber..."

"Then what the hell are you asking?" I asked him, trying to keep my voice down until I noticed the look of utter confusion in his expression.

"See? You don't even know what you want. You come back here and want to play around, but this isn't a game. This is my life—this is my little girl's life. You can't come back to Palmer, have your fun and then go away again. And we both know that's what you're going to do. So let's just cut our losses and move on."

"Amber, you have to believe me when I say that's not my intention. I am not playing a game. I know I have a life in Austin and I'm supposed to go back, but that doesn't change how I feel about you... how I've always felt about you."

I wanted to cry out in frustration, but laughed out sarcastically instead. "You have a funny way of showing me how you feel about me, Liam," I said, regretting having come over here, and instantly knowing the hurt in his eyes would haunt me that evening when I got home.

"Then let me show you the right way," he said in a low voice, and before I realized what he intended he stepped into my space, cupped my jaw, bent his head and laid a kiss on me I felt all the way down to my toes.

I should've pulled back, been more aware of my surroundings, but I got lost in his kiss. It wasn't until I felt his hand skate down my back and over my hip that I gained enough sense to pull away.

I glanced around wildly at the remaining party guests. The shadow of the tree had hidden Liam and me, so as far as I could tell, no one saw us. I needed to get out while I still could.

I shook my head at him. "I can't do this with you, Liam... not again."

Then I turned on my heel and headed back across the lawn.

When I came inside the house to pack up, Sheila was ushering a group of guests out the door.

"Sheila, if it's okay with you, I'll begin cleaning up."

"Of course, Amber, we want you home before the storm hits. Oh, I could just kill that meteorologist, absolutely no mention of this," she groused. "But I have to tell you how wonderful the desserts were. I have some more names to email you who asked about your availability."

I grinned proudly. I couldn't let my fight with Liam overshadow tonight's success.

"That's amazing, Sheila. I look forward to connecting with them."

"Wonderful!" she enthused. "And I want to talk to you about a holiday party. I know it's still early, but I want to make sure I secure a spot in your schedule because it appears you're about to be very busy," she said, smiling.

I couldn't believe it. I pulled it off... so why didn't I feel better? There wasn't much to cleanup. The wait staff had packed most of the remaining desserts, but I cleared away what I could and loaded it into my car.

I needed to get out of there as quickly as possible, otherwise I'd be tempted to go back and talk to Liam. I don't know what I thought I was going to accomplish if I went back to talk to him because, honestly, there was nothing left to say. Yet I kept thinking about the hurt in his eyes as he watched me walk away.

Serves him right. He should know what it feels like to have somebody walk away from him.

Even as I thought the words, I didn't take any satisfaction in them. I hated the hurt in his eyes, and it was taking everything in me not to go fix it.

"Just get your butt home," I muttered to myself as I piled the last of my belongings into the car and settled into the driver's seat.

It was sprinkling now and by the time I made it a mile away from the Rockefeller's, the skies had opened up and it was pouring. There was little to no visibility, so I threw my hazards on and made my way slowly towards home.

I nearly jumped out of my skin when a crash of thunder sounded overhead. "That was way too close," I said to myself as I leaned forward in my seat, trying to see as best as I could. Finally, the rain subsided enough that driving the last mile home was bearable. Hopefully, that was the worst of the storm, and Palmer wouldn't see too much damage. We had a rough winter, and many houses in town needed repairs. The last thing we needed was a severe storm to come through to undo all the progress people had made.

But as I pulled up to my house, my worry for others quickly turned to devastation for myself. The large oak tree on the south side of the house had fallen—and punctured a hole in the roof right over the kitchen.

"Oh, my God," I murmured repeatedly to myself as I jumped out of the car, not caring that the rain was drenching my beautiful dress.

I ran inside the house to see what I feared most. The roof over the kitchen was completely caved in, and the tree had made its way inside. The rain poured down on all our things—on our whole life.

"Oh my God, what am I going to do?"

I couldn't even cry, I was so stunned. I just stood, staring at the devastation. Thankfully, Abigail was with her grandmother right now, and she hadn't been here when this happened. "And there goes my shop," I said to myself quietly, and then the tears came and I couldn't stop them.

I sank down to the ground on my knees, the water still raining down on me as I eyed the enormous hole in my roof. Even with the money I made from the party that night, it wouldn't begin to cover the damage that had been done. Not to mention I now didn't have an operational kitchen.

I don't know how long I knelt there. It felt like an eternity, but it had to only have been a few minutes.

I didn't know what to do. It was like I was frozen, but then a familiar voice brought me back.

"Amber! Amber, where are you? Please be okay. Please tell me you're okay?" A panicked voice came through the door.

Liam.

LIAM

T he sight that met my eyes when I came upon Amber's house had my heart launching into my throat. All I could hear was the pounding in my ears. I couldn't even hear myself screaming her name.

When I heard her teary answer, "Liam, I'm here," I almost fell to my knees. When I finally located her sitting on the ground, now wet from the water still pouring down from the enormous hole in her roof and her face wet with tears and rain, I fell to my knees in front of her.

Before I could stop myself, my hands were reaching for her face, feeling over her head, her cheeks, her neck and over her shoulders. "Are you okay? Are you hurt?"

She struggled to speak through her tears. "I'm okay, I'm not hurt... except for that," she said miserably, looking up at the massive crater in her roof.

"Hey, I get it—it's overwhelming, but don't worry, we're going to get this place fixed up. I'm just relieved you're okay, and that Abigail wasn't here and..."

She was nodding. "I am too, I know. I'm so glad she's with my mom right now, but Liam..." she stopped, hiccupping. "This is where I run my business. Everything I turned myself inside out working so hard for just went up in smoke. There's no way insurance is going to cover all of this and I will not have a kitchen to use even if I use my mother's. Her condo barely has a kitchenette," she ranted miserably.

She let me pull her into my arms and I let her sob onto my shoulder.

I tried to give her encouraging words. "Amber, it's going to be okay. We're going to figure this out."

But every time I told her what I thought were consoling words, she sobbed harder into my shoulder. I couldn't shake the feeling that the sobs were for much more than the huge hole over our heads and the rain pouring down on us. Her cries were old and primal and it felt like she was mourning much more than the loss of a roof.

We sat on the cold, wet ground for a long time in each other's arms, until her cries subsided to soft little sniffles, when she finally pulled her face from my chest and now sopping shirt.

I loathed the loss of contact, but I was relieved to see her look up at me without a fresh wave of tears taking over. She was finally calming down from the shock of everything.

"I appreciate you coming out to check on me Liam, but I've got it from here," she said resolutely. Then she pulled away completely to stand on slightly wobbly legs since we'd been sitting for so long.

"What? That's it?"

She looked down at me with determination in her eyes. "I'm not sure what you were expecting."

"I don't know. You went from being hysterical to kicking me out. If you want me out, fine, although I don't think that's a good idea, do you?"

The words were barely out of my mouth before I knew I said exactly the wrong thing again.

"I am quite accustomed to handling things on my own, thank you very much. I appreciate your care and concern, but I can take it from here."

"But you don't have to."

Her eye twitched, and I couldn't decide if she was going to cry again or if she was going to haul off and hit me. Honestly, I would have welcomed either over this cold, resolute, stiff woman who seemed so determined to get me away from her.

I could really be stepping in it now, but I forged a head saying, "I realize I probably did this."

A shock expression stole over her features before she returned her expression to neutral and played it down. "What? You're responsible for the hole in the roof? You can take credit for a lot of things, Liam, but you can't take credit for that one."

"Don't do that. Don't act like you don't know what I'm talking about. I understand you don't want to talk openly about what happened between us, and I'm probably largely responsible for the tough spot you are in right now. As much as it pains me, I take ownership of it. But Amber, I am here right now, and I can help you. You should let me help you—if not for you, then for Abigail."

"Just how do you propose to help me, Liam? There's nothing you can do. I'll call the insurance company tomorrow and clean up the mess and..."

"I will help you clean up the mess and make sure you have someplace to stay and a kitchen to bake in," I cut in.

She laughed. "There's no need for that. We'll stay with my mom."

"You just told me your mom is in a tiny little condo and there won't be room for you. Not to mention you need someplace to bake. I saw all those cards you collected tonight. Are you really going to let that go to waste because of stubborn pride?"

"Where do you expect me to go, Liam?" She said, waving her arms around wildly.

"Come home with me," I said before I could lose the nerve.

She stood there stunned with her mouth open before she recovered and let out a mirthless laugh. "That's the most ridiculous thing I've ever heard."

"Why? Pop's house is huge. There's plenty of space for you and Abigail and you would hardly have to deal with me. I'll be too busy over here fixing this mess." I saw her hesitate, so I pressed on, "You know how big Pop's kitchen is. You could probably take on more clients with the extra space."

"What am I supposed to tell my little girl? That we're moving into a man's house she just met?"

"I know she's been in Pop's house before. Her art is plastered everywhere... pictures of you both, too," I added without thinking, then almost immediately kicked myself when I saw the befuddled expression on her face.

"Look, if it makes you feel better, I'll stay here while this is getting fixed and you guys can take Pop's house."

She shook her head vehemently. "No, I couldn't have you stay here while we take over Patrick's house."

That didn't surprise me. "Look Liam, I appreciate the offer but..."

"Don't say no yet—think about it for a little while." I said as I moved toward the kitchen. "Where do you keep your trash bags?" I asked her. She started to argue, but I wasn't having it. "Look, I'll let you think about whether you want to stay in Pop's house or not, but I'm helping you clean this up. It's nonnegotiable, Amber."

She sighed, her shoulders slumping in defeat. "They're under the sink."

I went to where she directed, grabbed the box of bags, and started shoveling the debris inside. It was late, and the rain had finally stopped. There was just the occasional drip now through the hole.

Once we had the worst of the debris bagged up, I planned to drive back to my dad's house and grab some tarps from his shed to cover the hole.

Amber joined in with me and we worked side-by-side in silence for a long time.

Finally, I couldn't take the quiet anymore. It was like I could practically hear her heart breaking and her mind spinning out over how she was going to handle all of this. I wondered once again how often she was stuck in a position where she had to manage everything by herself.

It was obvious her mom helped where she could, but the weight of the world was on Amber's shoulders, and I wanted more than anything to bear the burden with her.

Suddenly, I felt guilty for all those years I'd been away. It was one thing to be heartbroken because I missed her, but I'd been living fairly footloose and fancy-free. There'd been no children to worry about and with the business success I enjoyed, I hadn't had to worry about keeping a roof over my head or food in my stomach. The biggest burden I carried was missing Pop and ruminating over the colossal fuck up I had made by leaving her.

So I broke the silence with a laugh. "Hey, do you remember the time the homecoming game got rained out, and we got stranded out by the concession stand?"

She stopped then and pondering, before finally relenting and saying, "I remember you trying to look all cool in your leather jacket, but you looked more like a drowned rat. Wasn't that your pompadour era?"

I laughed as I remembered, "Hey, I thought I could be the reincarnation of Elvis. And you're the one who told me I looked exactly like him when I did those dance moves."

She rolled her eyes with a reluctant smile. "I only told you that, so you'd keep singing his songs to me. It was the only way I could get you to do it. You were too embarrassed otherwise."

"Was that your trick?" I said, stepping in close to her, leaning on the broom in my hand. "I haven't sung since high school."

"What? You don't serenade your construction crews?"

I laughed, "Please, I would have a nail gun tossed at my head."

It was so good to hear her laugh. I'd forgotten how it had a way of wrapping around me and making me do anything to hear it again and again.

After a moment of hesitation, she mumbled, "That's a shame."

"I guess we drop a lot of hobbies we pick up in high school. Did you ever finish knitting that sweater?"

She barked out a laugh. "Oh my God, the ill-fated sweater. I wish I would have known then about the boyfriend curse."

I raised an eyebrow in question, and she continued. "Apparently, the quickest way to end any relationship is to knit a sweater for your boyfriend. I didn't know about it at the time, but somebody told me later on. No, if you must know, I think the sweater is up in the attic somewhere only a quarter of the way done. If you can even call it a sweater—it ended up being a big tangled ball of yarn, really."

I didn't comment on the boyfriend curse. I remem-bered that sweater well. It was hideous, but she had worked so hard on it and was so excited to be making me something. I was fortunate she wanted to make me anything at all—especially something that took so much love and effort. If I had stayed, and she had finished it, I probably would've worn that ugly-ass sweater anytime the temperature dropped below fifty degrees.

We stopped and looked at each other for a long moment. I couldn't help but think about all the memories I had been avoiding—particularly the ones that were as sweet as they were painful. I couldn't bear to remember them, so I pretended they never happened. But looking at Amber now, I realized that a whole lifetime happened in the short time we'd been together and it was nice to relive them with her.

She broke our gaze by looking around at the mostly swept floor. "I think that's the worst of it for now. I suppose it's time to get a tarp up there," nodding up to the ceiling.

"Right, I'll go grab those from Pop's house. I don't want to leave you here alone, though."

She shook her head, "It's fine, and I don't want to leave this place unattended. I can't imagine anyone messing with it, but you never know."

"Okay, I'll be back as soon as I can. But call me if anything happens."

She nodded in agreement. As I drove away, she watched me until I couldn't see her anymore in my rearview mirror. I recalled another time I'd watched a worried Amber in my rearview mirror, but this time it wouldn't take me thirteen years to come back.

As I paced my house, I tried not to look at the gaping hole in my ceiling. My mind was swimming with worries—and questions like could I make it work living with Liam at Patrick's house?

I didn't have too long to focus on it because in a matter of fifteen minutes, Liam was back as promised with the tarps. Between the two of us, we fished the ladder out of my old shed and I nervously watched as he climbed the ladder that was now sinking into the mud alongside the house.

"Please be careful," I said.

"Don't worry," he assured me, "I only do this every day," he said, looking down over his shoulder with that handsome smile of his, and there was a flutter in my chest, which I found wholly inconvenient.

He expertly threw the tarps over the hole and he was right—he looked like he did this every day.

Once the hole was covered up, we went back inside the house, and I began packing things out of the way. I didn't know how this was going to work. My gut reaction was to say no to Liam's offer to stay at Patrick's house, but a tiny part of me entertained the notion. The house had an impressive kitchen, whereas mom's condo had a microwave, fridge, and a compact range.

As much as I loved my mom and I know she loves us, she had her routine, and I couldn't predict how long we would need to stay.

And those business cards were burning a hole in my purse since I'd received them from Sheila's friends. If I lose those opportunities, opening my own shop would definitely be off the table and I'd be lucky to keep my business afloat at all. It would be like starting all over again, and I don't think I have that kind of energy in me anymore.

Suddenly, the events of the day crashed into me all at once and I stopped my frantic pacing, turning around in a slow circle to look at the chaos before plopping down into a soaked easy chair.

"Amber?" Liam asked behind me, and then his big, reassuring hand was on my shoulder.

"I'm okay, I'm just exhausted," I admitted.

"I bet," he sympathized.

We had been at this for hours now, and I had been running on pure adrenaline for most of the day. I felt like I could collapse at any minute.

"What time is it?" I asked.

He looked at his wrist to check. "Quarter after five. You need to get some sleep, Amber. Let me take you home."

His words were so tempting and his voice so alluring, but I didn't get the feeling he was trying to be either of those things. He was just being the guy his father raised him to be.

"You make it sound so easy," I said, turning to look at him.

And that's when I noticed the bags beneath Liam's eyes. I'd been so caught up in what was happening to me, I hadn't stopped to notice that this man had rushed here in the middle of a storm to make sure I was alright and was now stuck to my side like glue to help me clean this place up and protect it from further damage.

I felt a tinge of embarrassment at my behavior. I was so focused on protecting my heart that I was lashing out at someone who'd been nothing but good to me since he'd returned to town. My guard was slipping, especially when he looked down at me and said, "It doesn't have to be hard, Amber... I know that's what you're used to, but it doesn't have to be that way."

It was all too much—too many setbacks, too many emotions. Too many moments where I just wanted to reach out and touch him. He'd always been so great in a crisis and obviously that hadn't changed. It made me want to feel his arms around me, and for once I didn't overthink my impulse. I did what my body urged me to do.

I stood up, slipped my arms around his waist, and tucked my head against his chest, instantly reassured by the steady beating of his heart. He slowly wrapped his arms around me and pressed me closer. I inhaled him in, taking what I guessed to be the first deep breath since this complete nightmare of a night started.

"I don't know what I'm going to do, Liam."

"I know it feels insurmountable Amber, but I promise you this is a blip on the radar. Sure, the night ended terribly, but think about the rest of the evening. Your cake was a smashing success, and all of those ladies want your business. I know you're wondering how you're going to make it all happen, but the answer is right there—you just have to grab it."

I snorted at his pep talk. Leave it to Liam to make this all seem like no big deal. Nevermind that a few weeks ago, I reached out to grab him and I'd found myself in a world of trouble. While our night together was incredible, I'd been paying for it ever since. Thinking about it had been an endless distraction, and now I contemplated what a life with him would be like.

There was nothing but heartbreak in that kind of thinking.

I was too tired to protect my heart now when his arms felt so good around me. I put my head back far enough to look into his eyes and whispered, "Liam."

I don't know what I was planning to do next, because I heard a car door slamming and then the quick steps of little feet running towards me.

"Mommy?" Abigail called out and before I could disentangle myself from Liam, my mom and Abigail stood in the doorway, looking at us curiously.

"Oh my word," Mom breathed, looking first at me, then at Liam and then at the roof over the kitchen, or what used to be the roof over the kitchen.

Abigail tore away from her grandmother's side and launched herself at my legs. "Mommy, I heard the storm, and I was so scared," she said, hugging me. Abigail was never a fan of storms. During every thunderstorm, she'd find her way into bed with me.

"I tried to calm her down, but she was so worried about you, I finally promised her we would go home early to check on you."

Abigail was clinging to me, her arms wrapped around my thighs and her face pressed to my hip as I stood still in Liam's arms. When I pulled back, he reluctantly let me go.

I bent down to Abigail and took her into my arms. "Sweetheart, I'm okay. The house is a little worse for wear, but I'm fine."

"I don't care about a stupid old house," she said, shivering in my arms.

I felt a pang of guilt. It never feels like I'm in the right place for Abigail. I should've been with her, but I was also so grateful she had not been in the house when this happened. If I thought she was scared of thunder before this...

"Where are we going to go, Mom?" she asked, looking up at me with concern in her eyes.

"Oh, well, I haven't quite figured that out yet," I said, peeking over at my mother, who looked confused. "I'm going to need a kitchen. I have quite a few bookings thanks to the party," I explained.

"Mother nature sure has great timing," my mom whispered.

That's when Liam chimed in. "The offer still stands, Amber. Come stay at Pop's house and put his kitchen to good use."

I looked up at him in warning, but it was too late. Abigail seized onto that idea with relish. "We could stay at Uncle Patrick's house? Mommy, let's do that. His house is so cool."

"Honey, I'm not sure that's a great idea. I don't want to be a bother to Mr. Liam."

"That's very gracious of you, Liam," my mother cut in, "but it wouldn't be appropriate."

There was something about that last word that made my hackles raise. I'd never given a lot of credence to what was considered appropriate or not. It was definitely something my mother had been hyper-focused on since I was a child. I was all for manners and even some etiquette, but I'd never given any thought to what Palmer had to say about me, and if I had, I would've withered from embarrassment ages ago. It was a town full of hard-working people who understood that everybody was trying to do the best they could to survive.

"What? It's not like anything unseemly would go on. Abigail could have whatever room she wanted and I could sleep on the couch if that would make everyone more comfortable. Heck, I'll stay here while you all stay at my dad's house," he offered again, making me want to punch him.

I knew what he was doing. It was one thing to offer this to me privately, but he knew Abigail was sold on the idea, and I sensed he was trying to stick it to my mother.

"Mommy, we couldn't have him stay here with a big hole in the house. Why can't we stay with him? And we could go out on that trail every morning."

The panic that had been seeping through my veins for the last several hours was giving way to pure exhaustion, and I would blame that when I started relenting. "Abigail, sweetheart, if we were to do this, we wouldn't stay for long. Just until this house was fixed."

"I know, but we can enjoy it until then," she said with her eyebrows raised and in her most convincing voice. It's the same voice she used around Christmas time when she went over her long list of desires.

I sighed, looking down into the hopeful face of my daughter and carefully avoiding the consternation on my mother's face. Finally, I looked over at Liam. He had an equally hopeful look in his eyes.

With a heavy sigh, I relented, "Okay, but only until the house is fixed," I insisted as Abigail started jumping up and down and Liam grinned. He bent down to Abigail and gave her a high five. It unnerved me how quickly they'd gotten into cahoots with one another.

"Amber, surely you can't think this is a good idea," my mother hissed in my ear as I stood at the foot of my bed, throwing clothes into a suitcase.

"Of course I don't, Mom, but it's the best option we have, and it won't be for long. Liam's going to help repair the damage to the house, and he's always been an efficient worker. I have no doubt we'll be back here in no time," I told her and hoped to God she couldn't tell I was lying through my teeth.

Truth be told, I didn't know how long this was going to take. Liam fixed things pretty quickly, but I couldn't have been the only one to sustain damage through the storm, and the insurance companies were known for dragging their feet.

I couldn't stop and shut everything down because Mother Nature had its way with my home and my workplace.

Liam was right about one thing—I earned so many opportunities the night before, and it would be foolish to not cash in on them. It was a big moment for my business, and I would not let it be washed away with the rain.

So I was going to have to put on my big girl pants and figure out how to share a dwelling with Liam Murphy.

The idea would've thrilled a younger me, but now it terrified me. I didn't think for one second Liam would do anything untoward, but I wasn't so sure about myself.

Standing in his arms right before my mom and Abigail showed up, the thought had crossed my mind how easy it would be to kiss him, to feel the comfort and excitement of his soft lips against mine—to recreate the night we'd had. That would feel amazing and help me forget my worries for a little while, anyway.

As much as my body was screaming for a do-over, I was grateful Mom and Abigail had shown up when they did.

"Surely, there's another solution to this problem," my mother said.

I stopped, unable to hear any more of her worrying and doubting. I knew her heart was in the right place, but in this moment, it was just fuel to the fire. "Mom, I know you mean well, but I need you to not doubt every single decision I make for my daughter and myself. I'm doing the best I can, and I don't need somebody second-guessing me every step of the way."

She looked hurt, and I instantly regretted the words. "Mom, I'm sorry. It's been an endless day. I've gotten no sleep, my roof is toast and..."

She was nodding, blinking back tears. "I understand, sweetheart. Believe it or not, I do. I just worry for you, that never stops as a parent, you know. But you are a grown woman and you're going to make your own choices, whether I like them or not," she said curtly. Then added quietly, "I don't want him hurting you again."

I nodded, understanding her concern. "Don't worry, Mama, no one will hurt me like that ever again," I assured her, even though we both knew it was a lie.

I had had a whole other life since Liam left, but the man waiting for me out in my living room still had the power to shatter my heart.

In my gut, I knew he wouldn't intentionally do anything to hurt Abigail. It was my heart I had to worry about.

But my heart might have to take a beating if it means I could open my own shop and make a better life for Abigail and myself. With that thought in mind, I packed my bags along with Abigail's and tossed them in the truck before we followed Liam back to Patrick's house.

The sights and sounds of Patrick's house in the mountains were instantly comforting and went a long way to soothe my trepidation about being there with Liam.

Once we entered the house, Liam told Abigail she could pick whatever room she wanted, and she made a beeline for a room towards the back of the house that she had played in many times before. It had two large windows that overlooked the foothills and she used to stare out of them endlessly, telling me about the fairies out in the brush.

Patrick had fed into this fairytale, putting out twinkly lights in strategic places in the brush and telling her when they lit up, it was the fairies coming out to play.

I think she figured out what he had done for her, but she played along just the same.

"I guess I'll take the room next to Abigail's, if that's all right."

"You can have the room I'm staying in. The bed is bigger and more comfortable," Liam offered.

"Liam, you're already offering us your house. I'm not going to take your bed too."

Heat lit his eyes, and he opened his mouth to say something, but thought better of it. I could feel a flush creep up my neck. That's when I remembered our kiss under the tree earlier that evening. With all the chaos of the storm and the house, I'd given little thought to how I'd almost given into him again.

I stiffened my spine. "I'll take my bags and make sure Abigail is settled in."

I trudged down the hall to the room next to Abigail's and set our bags down.

The room was exactly as Patrick had left it, with a full-size bed and an old quilt his mother made for him covering the foot.

It looked so inviting—I was so exhausted.

I went next door and popped my head into Abigail's room to see she was already lining up her toys and starting some sort of game having to do with fairies and horses.

"Are you okay, sweetie? Do you need anything?"

She looked at me with bright eyes and smiled as she shook her head no.

"I'll be right next door if you need me. Okay?"

"Yes, mama."

With that, I drifted back into "my room" and the inviting bed. I could lie down for a few minutes to rest, but then I needed to start unpacking and call the insurance company.

At least that's what I told myself before I closed my eyes, and that was the last thing I remembered.

LIAM

Amber slept... and slept... and slept.

When Abigail emerged from her new "room" she told me she was hungry but her mommy was asleep. I fixed her a grilled cheese sandwich, and we ate lunch together. "It's been a long couple of days for your mom. She needs rest."

Abigail nodded in agreement. "She works too much, but I know she likes what she does, so I guess it's okay."

Abigail proceeded to tell me about the fairy action going on behind the house and all the lights Pop had set up for them.

I grinned, "that sounds like my dad. Maybe we should go out there to see if any of the fairies are still hanging out. They need to know their queen is back in town," I teased her.

So I spent the day playing with Abigail, checking on Amber periodically, and she was laid out like a stone. I know she's been burning the candle at both ends, so I let her rest.

By the time the evening rolled around, I had Abigail settled in the living room where she was playing with her horses on the coffee table, and I found a DVD copy of the Minions, which made Abigail's eyes light up. "Uncle Patrick let me watch that when I was here," she informed me.

"Well, no sense in breaking tradition," I told her as I slid the disk into the DVD player. "I'm going to go start dinner for us. Holler if you need anything, okay?"

"Yep," she nodded happily. She really was an easy-going kid, a lot like her mother was when she was younger—not so much now.

The kitchen was an open concept. There was a bar-top with an opening so I could see through to the living room and keep an eye on Abigail. It was so gratifying watching her curly mop of hair bouncing along as she played with her horses and watched her movie, and it felt so natural for me to be making her dinner while her mom slept.

I turned away, suddenly feeling stinging at the back of my eyes. The last thing I needed to do was start bawling like a big old baby in front of Abigail. That would no doubt freak her out, and her mom would likely be upset with me, too. But it hit me—everything I had given up when I believed Sandra's lies.

If only I had more confidence or the courage to fight for Amber and tell her she was wrong. But she was very convincing when pleading her case that Amber would be better off without me.

I wrestled with a renewed surge of anger towards Sandra as I prepared dinner. It was nothing fancy, just burgers on the stove, but it was Pop's recipe with his "secret spices" which made them unexplainably addictive. I hoped Abigail would like them.

We were sitting at the kitchen table, about to take our first bites of the burgers, when Amber appeared at the mouth of the hallway, bleary-eyed and slightly disheveled. "What time is it?" She asked weakly.

I smiled at her, "Well good evening, nice to see you sleepyhead."

"Yeah, hi sleepyhead," Abigail chimed in.

"It's a little past six," I answered her question.

Amber's eyes widened. "I only meant to rest my eyes for a second. I didn't mean to fall asleep for twelve hours," she said, her voice rising with each syllable.

"It's okay, you needed the rest, and Abigail and I had a good day here."

"I showed him where the fairies are, Mom and he told me he could build them their own little miniature treehouse to match the one in the backyard... although I guess everything's kind of their treehouse, right?" She asked, looking thoughtful.

Amber's look of dismay at having been asleep for so long gave way to an adoring smile towards her daughter. "I suppose you could make that argument," she said, moving closer to us.

"Well, come on over here and eat. You must be starving and there's more than enough for everyone," I told her, beckoning her to the table with a plate.

I watched her cute little nose sniffing, "Are those Patrick's burgers?" she asked, and I smiled at her recollection. This was the same meal Pop had made us every time I brought her home when we were kids, and from the way Abigail had responded, I had a feeling he'd fixed them for her a few times as well.

"Sure are, although I can't claim they're going to be as good as Pop's, but I did my best."

Abigail took a big bite out of her burger and contemplated. "They're not exactly the same, but they're good. Good job, Liam," she said, giving me a thumbs up as she continued digging into her food.

"Well, if you got her stamp of approval, they must be pretty good," Amber said, sitting down and grabbing a plate.

This was so easy, relaxing even. So this is what I've been missing out on for so long.

Maybe you don't have to miss out on it any longer.

The voice in my head was not my own. It was sure and steady—the voice that had been guiding me since I was born. I knew in that moment Pop had played a part in all of this.

"Liam? Are you okay?" Amber asked.

I swallowed around the lump that had formed in my throat. "Yeah, I'm fine—I was just remembering something about Pop," I admitted.

She nodded with understanding. "We miss him too."

Abigail chimed in. "Don't worry, he's still here," she said matter-of-factly.

Amber and I looked at each other, but didn't say anything.

Abigail might be right.

Amber

A bigail and Liam were like two peas in a pod and I had some seriously mixed feelings about it.

I was glad Abigail was so comfortable with him and it was heartwarming to see how good he was with her, much like his father had been. But I was worried I was setting us up for heartache.

It didn't help that my mom kept checking in on us, offering other suggestions of where we could go. But I wasn't about to move Abigail again. She was settled in here, and I don't think wild horses could drag her away from the fairy garden outside her bedroom window.

So we would stay put until our house was livable again.

First thing Monday morning, I put on my headset and to call the insurance company while I made my nearly daily trip to the grocery store for ingredients so I could start on my next order. I had several meetings scheduled over the next few days with women I met at Sheila's party. It would be busy, but I was so excited about the prospect of opening my very own shop that I was up for the challenge.

But first, I needed to move all of my equipment to Liam's kitchen. Once I was done at the grocery store, I'd swing by the house to grab what I'd left in the pantry and fridge.

I finally got to speak with a claims agent after a fitful bout of phone prompt hell and they'd helpfully informed me it would be several weeks before anyone could come look at the house. There'd been extensive damage in Palmer and several of the surrounding communities—and they were predictably short-staffed.

When I'd asked them how in the world I was supposed to live in my house with a gigantic hole in my roof, they'd helpfully suggested I could "take care of it myself out of pocket."

"Shit," I muttered quietly as I tossed my groceries in the trunk and headed back to my house.

I tried to not get too frustrated. I would find a way around this, I coached myself as I pulled up to the front of my house, only to discover Liam's truck out front. Abigail was safely at school, so I guess I it shouldn't have surprised me to see him there. I was, however, surprised to see him on the roof.

As I got out of the car, he grinned down at me broadly, "Oh hey, fancy meeting you here."

"Liam, what are you doing? I just got a hold of the insurance people. You can't be up there yet..."

He moved his way to the edge of the roof and down the ladder. "Forget the insurance company. Like you said, they're going to take forever and I can get this fixed in no time."

"No, I can't ask you to do that."

He made a face. "Did you forget what I do for a living, Amber?"

"Of course not, but I can't afford the materials and..."

He turned away, heading back towards the ladder, "Don't worry about that, it's covered."

"No, listen, that's too much."

"Don't get all worked up. I made a few calls yesterday while you were sleeping. A lot of people owe me favors, so they overnighted all the materials we need. We're getting this done practically for free, my lady," he told me proudly.

I balked as I noticed the pallet of materials positioned next to my house. "I can't believe this," I breathed.

"Now, I know you want to be back in your house as quickly as possible, but I won't do a rush job. We need to make sure everything's dried out—the last thing we want is mold to grow."

"No, of course," I agreed, still somewhat breathless.

"Amber," he said, drawing my attention back to his face. "I told you it was going to be alright, and I meant that."

I blinked back tears and said, "I don't know how I'm going to repay you for this."

"You don't owe me anything, Amber." He said as he turned to climb back on the ladder.

Not knowing what else to do, I went inside the house and packed up my equipment I'd left the day before. I also made him lunch, so he wouldn't forget to eat when he took a break.

"When you have a moment," I called up to him, "I left a couple of BLTs for you in the fridge."

"BLTs? My favorite," he enthused.

"I know, I remember," I said, smiling. "I got to get to work, so I guess I'll be in your kitchen."

"I'll see you at home later, Amber."

I just nodded because honestly, I didn't know what to say to those words. All of this felt so surreal but as the days wore on with Liam working on my house, and me diving headlong into orders and meetings with new clients, it felt less surreal and more like reality—like the reality that Abigail and I should've had all along.

Living with Liam and Abigail felt like family—and a bubble I desperately did not want to burst.

For all the bitterness I'd held against this man all these years, I was nothing but grateful for what he was doing for me and my daughter. He wasn't just giving us a place to stay—it was a fun home and family experience. Every day when Abigail came home from school, Liam would make dinner for us and on more than one occasion, he helped Abigail with her homework.

One afternoon, she had come home from school, and he had a surprise for her out back. He told her he got to thinking about the fairy treehouse situation, and while the entire world was their treehouse, he thought they might need a nice little lounge area. So he'd made this little miniature deck and lawn chair set up and nestled it in the brush with some fairy lights for them to "relax their little wings" as he had put it.

Abigail was delighted, and I was ecstatic to see my daughter so happy.

With Liam working on the house, I made it a habit of bringing him lunch every day. It was the least I could do, all things considered.

I was on the way to my house with his lunch when I got a call from my mom. Upon asking what I was up to, I told her, "I'm taking some lunch to Liam. He's working on the house."

There was a strained silence. "What? Spit it out, Mom." I pressed.

"I just think you're getting awfully close to someone who has a history of running away, and now he's getting close to Abigail... and I don't like it, I don't like it one bit."

Suddenly, I couldn't take it from her anymore. "Mom, you have made your feelings known—on numerous occasions. But Abigail is happy and I am happy. He's been really good to us. Besides, he's not a kid anymore and people change. I know you're worried he'll break our hearts, but it's not like anything is happening between us. He's showing some kindness to an old friend and her little girl, and I'm grateful to accept it."

"That's how it starts," she said. "I saw the way you looked at him when I showed up at your house the other day. It's the same look you had when you were younger."

I didn't know what to say to her. She was probably right. I probably was looking at him all moony-eyed. Liam had that effect on me. But part of me hoped my defense of him wasn't in vain. He was a grownup, not the scared nineteen-year-old who left all those years ago.

He's only proven to be kind and considerate since he's been back in town. Even if he drove me nuts occasionally—which isn't really his fault, since all I want to do is climb him like a tree.

I was proud to admit I had resisted that impulse in the days we've spent with him.

When I arrived at the house, he insisted I stay to share it with him.

"Liam, I should get back to..."

"You should take a break every once in a while. I know you have these fancy new clients, but you're not going to be any good to anyone if you burnout. Now come help me eat this sandwich," he cajoled. As I opened my mouth to protest, my stomach grumbled.

"See, you need some nourishment. You're so busy taking care of everybody else that you forgot to take care of yourself," he grumbled as he cut the sandwich in half and handed half of it to me.

Begrudgingly, I took the other half. He filled me in on the details of the roof repair and I bounced some ideas off of him for my latest client creation.

I swallowed another bite of sandwich, then I told him, "I really appreciate you doing this. I might actually have a shot at opening my own store now."

"You will if I have anything to say about it," he promised. "Where are you wanting to set up shop, anyway?"

I smiled sheepishly. "Well, I need to find someplace reasonably priced..."

He made a tsking sound, "Now come on. That's not what I asked. Ideally, where do you want your storefront to be? I know you must have some dream spot in mind."

I looked at him cautiously. My mom, Abigail and Lena knew about the storefront. Otherwise, I kept that fantasy to myself. Real estate on Main Street was pricey, and it didn't seem realistic to hold out for it, although every time I closed my eyes and thought of my shop, I saw the space on the corner of Main Street.

He tilted his head quizzically. "I'll tell you what, I'm at a good breaking point with the roof today. And you need a serious break before you hit the cakes again. Why don't you show me," he suggested in a voice that made me want to show him a lot more than the storefront.

I hated to admit it, but watching him work away on the roof and eying the way his arms flexed with every strike of the hammer did things to me. And those visions had been burning in my brain every night before I fell asleep into an exhausted stupor.

I really should have gone back to work, but I smiled at him instead. "Okay."

His eyes lit up. "Well, let's go then! What are we waiting for?"

The next thing I knew, we were in Liam's truck, and I was directing him towards downtown.

"I think I might know where you're leading us to," he said with a small smile tugging at his lips. Without any further direction from me, he drove the truck straight to the front of what I had been my heart's biggest desire... until he breezed back into town.

Still, at the sight of the empty shop window, I got a fluttering in my chest.

But Liam wasn't looking at the storefront. He was looking at me, smiling. "This is it, ain't it?"

I nodded, trying to contain my excitement. "I don't know. It might be a little too far out of my reach."

He was shaking his head. "Oh, I don't think so. I can picture you with your bakery cases and a nice kitchen in the back. We could throw up a fresh coat of paint on the walls. What are you thinking? Mint green? Sky blue? Some sort of bakery color, right?" He laughed, and I was laughing along with him.

When we were younger, I had schooled Liam on what the "proper bakery colors" should be—all of which were pastels. "I don't know, I'm leaning towards mint green. I'm kind of going for an old-school ice cream parlor vibe," I said, and then spewed out all of my visions for what it would look like inside and where I would set up every-thing, pointing to various spots through the window. He dreamt along with me, making suggestions about where certain things could go and how to lure more foot traffic to the corner.

"What you need is a big sign that wraps around the corner up top. I'm thinking about those old-school movie marquis signs. I know a guy in Austin who restores signs like that, so we could quite literally put your name up in lights. That oughta grab everybody's attention."

His enthusiasm for my dream warmed me, and I felt like we were kids again sitting in his truck, making plans for the future—in between make out sessions.

"I think you can do this Amber... you just have to believe that, too."

I let out a nervous breath. "Yeah... Maybe. I still have to scrape the money together. You know as well as I do that's not always easy."`

He opened his mouth and started to say something, but my phone started ringing. I looked down at the screen. "Crap, that's one of my clients. I have to take this," I said, answering the phone. Even though I was focusing on what my client was saying, I couldn't help but notice the anxious expression on Liam's face.

As soon as I ended the call, I continued, "I am so sorry. What were you going to say?"

He gave me a tight smile, "nothing, don't worry about it. I should get you back to the house so you can keep working to make this dream a reality."

I nodded, and he drove me to my car so I could get back to work.

Later that evening, as I was tucking Abigail into bed, I couldn't help but revel in the moment's peacefulness. With the house tucked into the foothills, there was a serene feeling at night before bed. The city lights twinkled off in the distance as mother nature and her inhabitants quietly drifted off to sleep.

I listened as Abigail said her prayers. She thanked God for her usual blessings: me, her grandmother, except now she added, "Thank you for Mr. Liam, and I pray we can stay here forever, amen."

I looked at her with an alarm. "Abigail, you know we can't stay here forever."

She looked at me dubiously. "Why not? We like Mr. Liam, and he likes us, and we all love the house. Why can't we?"

I hated this part. "Because this is not our house. It's not even going to be Mr. Liam's house for very long. He lives in Austin and he has to go back soon. He'll be selling the house to another family."

I hated the look of disappointment on her face, but she surprised me with her words, "Well then, I don't mind giving up the house if Mr. Liam can stay. We have room at our house, Mommy. Can he stay?"

I sighed, "Oh, honey, he doesn't live here."

"But he could," she said, digging in her heels.

I hugged her to me, "Oh, sweetheart. I know it's hard having to let someone go, but I'm sure he'll visit," I said, wondering if I just lied to my child.

But Abigail was not to be deterred. She looked at me like I was being difficult. "I don't know, Mama. I think he's going to stay."

The sound in her voice sounded like the case was closed. Sometimes her stubbornness reminded me of her grandmother.

"We'll see, baby," I told her softly, hoping we could change the subject. It was too late in the evening to upset her by trying to make her understand all of this would eventually end.

Later, when I left her room after she'd fallen asleep, I finally let the tears slip down my cheeks, grateful the dark hallway concealed me. Liam had already gone to his bedroom, so I padded quietly to my own, and let myself grieve for what couldn't be—even though I desperately wanted it. And this time, it wasn't just for me, but for Abigail, too.

LIAM

I didn't mean to eavesdrop on Amber and Abigail, but when I spied them through the crack in the bedroom door, I couldn't help but admire the sight of Amber with Abigail in her arms as Abigail said her prayers.

I'd gotten quite attached to that little girl over the last week and Amber... well, that attachment had never been severed, and it was reforming with a renewed strength that frightened me.

I'd spoken to Benny earlier that day. "I'm starting to think I'm going to lose you to Colorado," he joked, but turned serious when I didn't answer.

"Liam? Are you thinking about staying?"

"I didn't say that man," I told him, even though I could tell by the sound of my voice I wasn't being truthful.

"I guess things are going pretty well with Amber, huh?"

I laughed. "I didn't say that either... but seriously, things are pretty fantastic. Only my life's not here and..."

"Here's a newsflash for you. There's this thing called 'moving'. It's not like the old days where you picked a spot and stuck with it. People are more mobile these days, in case you missed the memo," he said sarcastically.

"Ha, ha." I let out a long sigh. "I still don't know if she would give me a second chance—I really hurt her, and her ex-husband is a real prick. I can't blame her for being gun shy, or overly protective of her daughter."

"But you wouldn't hurt her again, right?"

"Hell no. I know better than that now. And there's no way I'd leave Abigail behind like her dad did. Lord knows if ever got my hands on that guy, it would take military-like force to remove me. How could he leave these two behind? And what the hell was I thinking, leaving Amber?" I added.

"Look, at some point, you have to quit beating yourself up for what happened in the past. None of us is perfect—we all make mistakes. Instead of focusing on your past, maybe it's time to start planning your future. And maybe you should let Amber in on what you're thinking. It sounds to me like that was the problem last time. You didn't let her know what was going on in your head, so you left her to wonder."

He was right, of course, but telling Amber how I felt and what I wanted was terrifying.

When I saw her with Abigail saying her prayers, I couldn't help but overhear their conversation.

My heart nearly jumped out of my chest. I wanted so badly to rush in there and promise them both everything Abigail was asking for and then some, but I know that's going to be a hard sell for Amber. Not to mention the fact she had no idea how well I'd done for myself since I'd left Palmer.

It's a matter of habit that I keep my wealthy status to myself, and I almost told her when I took her by the empty shop. In fact, for the last several days, I'd been mulling over how I could buy it for her so she wouldn't have to worry about coming up with the money, and start building her dream.

But I also knew Amber well enough to know she would never accept that. As it is, it's a miracle she's letting me fix her roof. She is not the sort of woman to take handouts. And after everything that went down with her ex-husband, I could understand she would be worried if strings were attached. And, of course, there were strings attached.

I left her, but I never stopped loving her. I could say that openly to myself now, and I wanted her and Abigail with me. As much as I kept from her back then, I wasn't sure how well it would go over when I told her I wasn't a struggling carpenter, but that I ran a multi-million-dollar construction company that was thriving. That I could theoretically retire tomorrow, and live happily into old age without ever picking up a hammer again.

After I heard the exchange between Amber and her daughter, I quietly locked myself in my room, trying to keep myself from running across the hall to Amber's room and telling her everything. Pleading with her to let me do this for her, to make up for the lost years and make life easy for her and Abigail. And to let me love her.

I was still mulling over how to go about telling her about my secret and what I wanted now with her and Abigail as I finished up with repairs at her house the following morning.

The hole was patched and new shingles were on, but there'd been a lot of water damage. I brought in an industrial-sized blower to ensure everything dried out because the last thing I wanted was mold to take over. While that was running, I made other little repairs around the house I'd noticed. The toilet in the main bathroom needed a flapper replaced. The door knobs in a couple rooms were sticky and needed some grease and a few window cranks needed replacing. I wanted to make sure the house was ready for Amber and Abigail to return. Although if I had anything to say about it, they would stay with me, permanently.

I would fix Pop's house and make it a home again—I wouldn't be selling to another family.

It was a nice day, so I left the front door slightly ajar as I worked to let in the fresh air. I heard an unfamiliar voice and then a knocking. "Hello? Amber?"

I popped my head around the fan. "Who are you?"

The man looked at me smugly. "I should ask you the same thing. You are in my house, after all."

Anger was rising inside me. I had a feeling I knew who this man was, but it did not change that he was an intruder in Amber's house.

"Since you don't seem to understand English," the man taunted, "let me introduce myself. I'm Ethan, Amber's husband."

I bit back a laugh. "You mean ex-husband," I corrected.

Ethan narrowed his eyes at me, then eyed the significant amount of work that had been done in the house, along with my tools spread out everywhere. "I don't appreciate being spoken to like that by the help. You may think you've gotten to know my wife since you've been fixing her house, but you can forget about it. I'm home now."

I laughed then. "People in town were right—you really are a smug son of a bitch."

Ethan glared at me. "I wouldn't put a whole lot of stock in those idiots. The only reason I even bothered to visit here is because Amber loved it so much, although I cannot see why. The first chance I get, I'm going to talk her into leaving this shithole, and she and our daughter and I can have a fresh start. Why am I even sharing any of this with you?" He said, looking irritated, as he turned away.

"That's a good question. After all, I'm just the help. Let me formally introduce myself," I said. "I am Liam. Liam Murphy," I said, sticking out my hand.

Recognition flashed in his eyes as he left my hand hanging there, refusing to shake it. "I see. The old boyfriend swooping back in for sloppy seconds, huh?"

My anger was reaching a fever pitch. "Don't you dare talk about her that way."

Ethan laughed cruelly. "I'll speak however the hell I want to about her. She's my wife. She's nothing to you. You were kids when you last saw each other. Besides, from what I heard, you left her for greener pastures."

I stood my ground, looking at him through narrowed eyes. "That's right. I did it because I was young and stupid. What's your excuse?"

"I don't need to answer any of your ridiculous questions."

"No, you don't have to talk to me. But you have some explaining to do to Amber. It's bad enough you left her, but how the fuck could you leave Abigail behind?"

Ethan shoved a warning finger at me. "Don't you dare say my little girl's name."

That did it for me. The self-righteous indignation of a guy who knew he'd been an absent parent the last few years, but didn't care, was too much.

"Please. Don't act like a protective dad now when you haven't been around in years and haven't even bothered to check in on her. I'll can tell you Amber and Abigail are doing just fine without you—better off, I'd say. You can criticize me for leaving Amber, I deserve it. It was the stupidest thing I've ever done, but she wasn't my wife, and I certainly didn't leave a child behind."

Ethan started closing the distance between us, and my hands clenched into fists at my side, ready to go if he got any closer.

"You wanna act like a big man?" Ethan said, shaking his head around like a chicken.

"Don't need to," I said coldly.

"Listen here, you ignorant son of a..." Ethan started.

He was cut off by an irate Amber. "What the hell is going on here?"

Ethan reluctantly tore his gaze from me and slowly turned to face Amber, pasting on a smile so fake it made me want to tackle him to the ground. "Amber, I was worried when I didn't find you here. But I did find this stranger here who has quite the attitude, by the way."

Amber looked between me and then her ex-husband. "He's no stranger. I can't say the same for you. What the hell are you doing here, Ethan?" She said steel in her voice and I had to resist the urge to applaud.

That's my girl.

Ethan let out a long sigh, "I came here to talk," he looked over her shoulder at me and then back at Amber, "I would prefer to do that alone."

"Oh, no, no," I said. "You don't need to be alone with her. I don't trust you."

"Well, this is none of your business," Ethan argued again, but Amber stepped in between us.

"Okay, that's enough."

She looked at both of us sternly before telling her ex-husband, "If you want to talk, we can do so out on the front porch with the front door open." Then she turned to me. "I will be fine. Wait here, this shouldn't take long," she said, shooting a warning look at Ethan.

I wanted to plead with her to not give this fucker the time of day. But I understood she felt like she needed to hear him out because he was Abigail's father. And that's when another realization hit me. Here I was making plans for our future without checking in with Amber. I wanted us to be a family, but whether I liked it or not, Ethan would always be in the picture. I needed to be the bigger person, so I unclenched my fists, bit back my pride and behaved.

Even though I wasn't actively involved in the conversation, I hovered by the doorway listening in. I wanted to be nearby in case Amber needed me, and even though I knew she could handle herself, I didn't trust this guy as far as I could throw him. Ethan started in with his cloying sentiments, "Amber, baby, I know we left things on bad terms..."

But she wasn't having any of it. "Don't Amber baby me. You're right, we didn't leave things on good terms—you torched our lives in an instant."

Ethan sighed dramatically. "Fine, I guess I take responsibility for all of it... if it makes you feel better."

I didn't have to see them to know Amber was rolling her eyes. "Tell me why you're here so we can get this over with Ethan," she demanded.

There was a strained silence before Ethan said, "I want my family back. I made a mistake. I want to be in my daughter's life again—and your life again."

My heart was thudding in my ears as I waited for Amber's response, and as the silence stretched out, worry clinched at my insides. Then she spoke in a low, even tone that communicated she was not messing around. "You want back in our lives? Great. Tell me, what would that look like? Are you going to be floating in and out, upsetting our daughter? Are you going to leave me in a position where I have to explain to our daughter why her dad can't be a consistent presence in her life? Because I can tell you right now neither of those are going to work for us. You're either in or you're out, and as far as I'm concerned, that's a hard pass. You had your chance. I'm done playing games with you, Ethan. I need to set a good example for Abigail and I will not settle for someone who doesn't actually care about me."

"That's not fair Amber," he started, but she cut in.

"No. I'll tell you what's not fair. Unfair is leaving at a moment's notice when you were never actually fully present in your daughter's life. What's unfair is you waiting for everybody else to make things better for you while you loafed around looking for the easy way out. What's unfair is you took advantage of me and my kindness.

You and I don't work well together, but I'll tell you what is working—the life I built here with Abigail. She's is doing great. She's a happy and healthy little girl. My business is thriving—and we don't need you, Ethan. I won't tell you can't be a part of your daughter's life, but I will not put up with any of your bullshit. You got me?"

"I want to prove to you I'm a better man, Amber. I want to prove to you both that I'm worthy."

"Fine. Prove it. Knock yourself out. But you better be consistent—turning over a new leaf for a few days isn't going to cut it. In the meantime, you better tread lightly. And you better check with me before you try to see Abigail. I don't want her getting confused and upset."

"Hey, I am going to have a place in Abigail's life whether you like it or not," Ethan bit out, finally letting go of the vitriol he'd been holding back.

"And there he is," Amber said. "The old Ethan. I knew you weren't far away."

"I don't want to play games with you Amber," he snapped.

"You're the only one playing games, Ethan. Do you want to threaten me or do you want to do whatever it takes to get back into our lives? I am warning you now, you do not have a leg to stand on. If you want to see Abigail, you have to go through me, and you need to respect that process or we're gonna have a serious problem."

And then my hands were clenching into fists again. I wanted more than anything to rush out the door, grab that idiot by the collar, and show him how I felt about him. I couldn't stand anybody talking to her like that or threatening her, but something was holding me back. It's like an invisible hand was pressing against my chest, warning me to stay calm. Pop was intervening again, reminding me I couldn't let my baser instincts take hold in the situation.

Amber had the upper hand when it came to Abigail, so I couldn't come in beating my chest like a caveman and risk her losing any of her footing. No, my job was to protect her and Abigail at any cost. I might've spent the last few days dreaming about what that could look like, but now I knew with bone-deep certainty this was my mission.

I came home to settle Pop's estate, and inadvertently stepped into my rightful place in this life, and nobody could convince me otherwise.

Amber

Watching Ethan stomp away from my house, I felt a sense of foreboding.

Ethan didn't take no for an answer, and now that I had said it outright several times, I was worried about what kind of trouble he would stir up, and I hoped none of the mud he kicked up would land on Abigail.

It was time to put our shields up, as far as I was concerned. Palmer would figure out real quickly Ethan was back, and they'd never been much of a fan, so I knew he would have eyes on him, but I needed the people closest to me to know what was up. That meant calling my mom as soon as possible, which meant having an awkward conversation with Liam.

Except it wasn't nearly as awkward as I had expected. He was looking at me with determination in his eyes. "Amber, I don't want to step on your toes or screw anything up for you, but you give me the word, and I'll go beat his ass," he said in all seriousness, and I couldn't help but laugh.

"What is so funny? You know I could," he said in disbelief.

I patted him on the chest, fighting the instant comfort of the feel of him beneath my fingers. "Liam, I know you're more than capable. It was so intense for a moment I think I had to laugh to release some of the pressure. I'm hoping Ethan is just blustering like he usually does. Once he doesn't get his way, he'll probably leave town with his tail between his legs. That said, I can never be too cautious when it comes to Abigail, so I need to put everybody on alert."

He was nodding. "What do you want me to do?"

"Well, you're not gonna like this," I started, and he leaned in closer as if he needed to be as close to me as possible when I said, "nothing."

Frustration streaked across his face. "You're right. I don't like that answer."

"At least for now. If I need to call in a bruiser, you're on the top of my list. But for now, I have to rally the troops to make sure Abigail is okay, and I need to know I can count on you to be there for that. For as long as you're here, anyway," I added hastily. Here I was talking like he was going to stay in Palmer forever and we both knew once he'd wrapped up everything he came here to do, he'd be back to Austin and out of our lives like nothing had ever happened.

That thought had me backing away. "I'm sorry you had to deal with him. Hopefully, he stays away, but this is my problem. I can deal with it."

"You don't have to deal with it alone," he called after me.

I turned and smiled at him, not saying anything, then proceeded to my car.

Little does he know the sooner I accept I will have to deal with it on my own, the better. The time spent with Liam at Patrick's house had been sweet, a little too sweet.

He and Abigail and I felt like a proper family, and after what she prayed for the night before, I knew I was going to have to pull the plug on this whole situation sooner than later. She and Liam were getting attached to one another, and I didn't want to set my little girl up for heartbreak.

The roof was repaired, but Liam kept finding other things wrong with the house. It wasn't anything that made it inhabitable, so it was time to think about moving us back into our home.

I blinked back tears as I headed back to work and pulled out my phone, calling my mother, "Mom, Ethan is back in town..."

I threw myself into baking for the rest of the day—I couldn't afford for my emotions to take over. I needed to keep a clear head. Once I filled my mom in on what happened with Ethan, I called Lena, too. Since she ran the diner and heard all the gossip, she had the inside scoop on just about everything happening in town, so she would keep me posted on Ethan.

It's not that I didn't want Abigail to have a relationship with her dad, but I didn't want her to go through the pain of him coming and going so casually.

Later that evening, after I'd tucked Abigail into bed, Liam was waiting for me outside her door.

"I need to talk to you," he said, and dread threaded through me. Would this be the moment where he told me this was all too much and he would go back to Austin soon?

Nervously, I followed him back out to the living room.

He was sitting forward with his elbows resting on his spread knees, looking pensive.

"Would you just say whatever it is you need to say?" I finally said, needing to rip off the Band-Aid.

He looked at me nervously. "I don't want you to get mad at me or be offended."

"Spit it out, Liam."

"I want to pay for a lawyer to keep Ethan in check. I know you want him to have a relationship with his daughter, but he doesn't seem like the kind of guy who respects boundaries and maybe if we had some decent legal representation, he would have no choice but to respect those boundaries."

Relief washed over me—that was not what I was expecting.

"Liam, I appreciate the offer, but lawyers are expensive and..."

"So? I don't care about that, and it's well worth it to protect you and Abigail. Besides, it's been just me all these years. I can afford to take care of you and Abigail too," he insisted.

But I doubted that. While I knew he was running a small company with a friend down in Austin, I seriously doubted he had much leftover once they paid the workers. Construction was a competitive industry, especially in Texas. I knew he was doing well enough for himself, but lawyers' fees could eat through savings in no time. I knew that all too well.

"Listen, I appreciate your worry, but I think you may be jumping the gun here. Ethan is going to do one of two things: he's going to get frustrated he didn't get what he wanted right off the bat and leave, or he might actually pretend to try for a little while... though I doubt that will last, but that's what worries me. I can't stand the thought of him ingratiating himself to Abigail, providing her with a sense of security, and then bailing again. She's already had to go through that once with him. I don't want her to go through it again."

He scooted closer to me on the couch and put an arm around my shoulder, pulling me in for a hug. "I totally understand, Amber, and I will do everything in my power to help you with this. She shouldn't have to go through any of it. Nobody should. You're an exceptional mom, Amber, and I'm in awe of you."

I looked up at him. "You're too much sometimes, you know that? I mean, insisting we stay here with you, getting in your way..."

"You haven't gotten in my way, not once. I love having you both here," he stated, looking down at me sincerely.

I wanted to kiss him so badly, instead I continued. "Still, you have to pack up the house and get it on the market. You can't tell me we're not cramping in your style."

His arm slipped free of me. "I'm not really worried about that," he said, looking away.

"What's that supposed to mean?" I asked him, forcing him to look back at me.

He looked at me for a long moment without saying anything. "I don't know... it's felt like this is where I'm supposed to be ever since I came back. I mean, it hasn't exactly been easy, but I feel Pop everywhere, and it feels good to be back in this house. And being with you and Abigail... feels like home," he finished quietly.

My heart was racing. These were the words I'd dreamed about and yet they terrified me. "Liam, I..."

But he wasn't about to let me argue with him. Instead, he bent to kiss me, but there wasn't anything sweet about this kiss. For all of his sweet words, his kiss was demanding, possessive, and consuming.

His arms tightened around my waist, and it felt like he would never let me go. I missed that feeling—the feeling of total possession, completely saturated love. That was how it always felt when we were in high school, like nothing would ever come between us.

Intoxicated by his kiss and needy from the high emotions of the day, I leaned into his kiss, twining my arms around his neck and pulling him even closer, enjoying the growl that slipped from the back of his throat as my tongue dueled ferociously with his, tasting him like it was replacing my oxygen.

I almost cried out when he pulled away, panting and looking down at me with a mixture of lust and something else I was too scared to identify. "Amber," he whispered as he stood up, grabbing my hands and pulling me up. Much like I did when I led him to my bedroom in my house, he was now tugging me to his.

He pulled me into his bedroom and shut down the door softly behind us. As soon as the door clicked shut, Liam turned to me, hunger in his eyes as he lunged for me, taking my mouth, his hands quickly divesting me of my clothes. The urgency in his fingertips sent trails of fire down my skin that raced straight to my pussy. "Liam," I moaned against his mouth as he started trailing kisses over my cheek and down my neck.

I don't remember his clothes coming off. I just knew one second my fingers were ripping at them and the next he was standing before me, gloriously naked.

I stood back for a moment, licking my lips as I took in the magnificent sight of this man. Years in construction had kept him lean, his shoulders were wide, his arms muscular. My eyes trailed down to his sculpted chest and abs, to the fine trail of hair on his lower abdomen and finally to the proud erection jutting forward, begging me to touch it.

"Amber, you keep looking at me like that and this is going to be over before it begins," he warned in a low, husky voice.

I let out a soft laugh as I looked up at him and then dropped to my knees.

"Amber?"

I placed the palms of my hands against each one of his thighs and leaned forward. "Let me taste you again," I said, and I heard his breath catch in his throat as he watched me flick my tongue out against the tip of him. He hissed out in pleasure. This emboldened me more, and I swirled my tongue around him as I took him into my mouth inch by inch.

I moved my hands to the root of him and started stroking as my mouth worked over the velvety flesh stretched tightly over his hardness.

His fingers found their way to my hair, gripping gently as he helped urge my head back and forth. But just as I was getting into a rhythm, he pulled me off him, looking at me impatiently. "I need to be inside you, now," he said in a low voice, pulling me to my feet and stalking me across the room until I was backing up and falling against his bed with him, falling down over me, taking my mouth with his frantically, as he positioned himself in between my thighs.

I was already slick with desire for him and wriggled eagerly against him as he positioned his tip against my entrance. "So fucking hot," he said against my lips. "That hasn't changed Amber. You still drive me crazy. All I want is you... you're all I've ever wanted," he said, as he slid inside me, pumping in rhythmic strokes that had me burying my face against his neck to keep from crying out.

Abigail was a couple of doors away and a sound sleeper, but I couldn't risk it. My hands clutched onto his shoulders so I could press my face even harder against him, as I fought to keep my volume low. He held me close to him as he worked his body inside mine, whispering sweet endearments in my ear. "That it's my love, that's fucking it, you're perfect... this moment is perfect. I don't want it to end."

Later, I would tell myself those were words said in the heat of the moment, but I took them in greedily and begged him for more. And while I was more than satisfied as he made me come hard around him, shivering in his arms, it was a deep satisfaction that stole over me when I saw him tense against me, grinding his hips hard against mine, chasing his orgasm.

I loved knowing I could make him come like that. I loved knowing I could possess him so fully, even if only for a few minutes.

After, I wanted to soak up his presence while I still could. But my mind went straight to his words in the living room, and hope bloomed in my chest. Maybe after all this time, Liam was ready to come home, and if he stayed in Palmer, maybe my fantasy of having a family with Liam wasn't so far out of the realm of possibility.

The next morning, I woke up to the sound of doves in the trees outside. I stretched, satisfied, enjoying the sweet soreness in my muscles. Liam and I had made love well into the night until we finally succumbed to sleep for a few hours. I looked over to his side of the bed and saw he was gone.

Sitting up, I looked around, and then I heard his voice from the bathroom. I thought about my to do list for the day as I enjoyed the soothing sound of his voice, but then my ears started picking up his words.

"Yeah, I've got some business to take care of, so I'll be back down soon. I need to get the house taken care of and a few more things squared away... yeah, I know, that's the plan, but I'll sort all that out when I'm back."

Whatever shred of contentment I'd been experiencing evaporated.

Stupid girl.

I should've known better than to let myself think for one moment he'd been telling the truth the night before. Maybe he'd meant what he said then, but now in the light of day he was talking about going home and leaving me all over again.

I sat up in bed, fighting the urge to puke. That happened the last time he'd left, too. Once I realized he was gone for good, I remember being so upset in tears that I leaned over and upended my dinner. I didn't have enough in my stomach to do that now, but boy, did it feel the same.

I hurried out of bed to look for my clothes. I needed to get out of here... I needed to get Abigail and me out of here. What had I been thinking?

"Amber? What's going on? What's the rush?" Liam asked, coming out of the bathroom.

"The rush," I told him as I put my clothes on, "is I have too much to do today, and I need to get Abigail and I packed up and back home."

"Packed up? There's no rush, you can stay..."

"But isn't there, Liam? I just heard you tell whoever you were going to be back soon—and I know, I should've known better, but I let my daughter get close to you and now I'm going to have to explain to her you have to go. We should be back in our own house, anyway. I mean, I can't thank you enough for fixing it up, but you need to get back to your life."

"No, no, no, don't do that to me. Amber, you misunderstood. I was talking to my business partner. There have been some issues since I've been gone that we need to address, and then we can start moving my shares over to him. I will have to go back to Austin for a little while. It could take a few weeks to get everything ironed out, but..."

"Shares? I mean, I knew you had your own company in Austin, but that makes it sound—wait, what do you mean for a few weeks? What could possibly take that long?" I asked him, confused.

Liam's face reddened. "It's not a small company."

"Okay, so you did a little better for yourself than I thought. I mean, that's good."

"It's more than that, Amber. My business partner and I hit a construction boom in Austin and we cashed in. That's why I told you not to worry about how much the lawyer was going to cost. Amber, our company is worth $50 million. Once I sell my half to Benny, I can retire and we will be set for the rest of our lives. I could even buy you that storefront you've been dreaming about if you still wanted to work, though you wouldn't have to."

I put up a hand to stop him as I tried to process what he was telling me. "Wait a minute, you mean to tell me you're a multi-millionaire?" I asked.

He nodded solemnly.

"Are you kidding me? All this time you've been back, and you forgot to mention you're running a multi-million-dollar company?"

"I'm sorry. It's just not something I tell people about. It's not that big of a deal..."

"The hell it isn't."

He chuckled softly then. "I mean, I guess it can be. Lord knows it can change a lot of things, but..."

"No, Liam," shaking my head, "it wouldn't change a lot of things. It doesn't change anything. You lied to me."

He looked stricken. "What did you want me to do? Announce to you the second I saw you. 'Oh, by the way, Amber, I'm loaded now."

"No, of course not. But we have been... close for a while now. At least, I thought we were. Here I've been thinking we're both in the same boat struggling, and that's not how it is at all. I am on a boat and you're... on a yacht."

"Oh, come on, I'm not that kind of rich."

I laughed at him humorlessly, "You are that kind of rich, but that's not the point. I don't care that you have money—you're still just Liam. You're a guy who lies. I seem to have a knack for finding those men."

He shook his head in confusion.

"Don't you get it? You made a promise to me all those years ago, but that was a lie. Ethan made promise after promise, but those were all lies. And we're right back where we started, aren't we?"

"Amber, that's not..."

"No!" I cried out, holding back tears. Maybe somebody looking in from the outside wouldn't think this is a big deal, but I felt like I was eighteen all over again. I had bought into this man's promises back then, and it had all been a ruse. And I felt stupid now.

I'd been going on all this time about struggling to get by and assumed Liam understood what I was talking about, that he and I were on the same page. Now I felt like a damn fool.

"Maybe it doesn't seem like a big deal to you, and that's what worries me. The lie comes too easily for you... seems to come too easily for everybody. But I can't do it anymore. I can't put my daughter's happiness at risk," I said, shaking my head and swiping the tears from my cheeks.

"Amber, come on," he said, coming towards me, but I backed away.

"No, I won't hear it. Please stay away. Abigail and I will be gone by the end of the day. Please don't try to stop us."

I rushed out of the room blindly, heading towards my room, grabbing a bag, and throwing everything into it. I had to figure out how I was going to explain this to Abigail without falling apart.

Liam could look confused all he wanted, but it was perfectly clear to me: Abigail and I needed a sturdy foundation, not one built on promises, lies, and good intentions that always fell through. She and I had had more than enough of that to last us a lifetime.

LIAM

After everything, it was over, just like that.

I could go over and over in my head about what I should've done differently, but it didn't matter now. Amber had made up her mind and felt so strongly that she was doing what was best for her daughter. There was no talking her out of it.

I didn't know how I was going to handle watching them leave until Amber strongly suggested I not be at the house when they left. She was holding back tears as she explained it would be hard enough to explain this to Abigail, but if Abigail saw him looking miserable, it would make things worse.

Not wanting to make things any more difficult than they already were, I scooped my keys off the hall table and got in my truck. I sat for a time, staring at the front of the house. As long as Amber and Abigail were still in there, I was still home, but when I came back to it, it would be empty again... it would be empty forever.

I slowly backed out and sped off. I had to find a way to get through to Amber. Maybe if I gave her some time to cool off, I could drop by the house later to talk it through.

I drove into town, tears swimming in my eyes. As I passed the grocery store, I spotted a familiar form obliviously pushing her cart through the parking lot—Sandra.

I chuckled mirthlessly. "Guess you got your way after all, Sandra," I bit out as I drove past.

Part of me was tempted to keep driving, leave all my stuff behind, and go straight to Austin. But once again, an invisible hand was holding me back.

I wasn't sure I wanted to listen this time, but it was more insistent.

"All right, old man, I've been jerked around enough. I hope you know what you're doing," I told the sky.

AMBER

"I don't understand! I hate you!" Abigail screamed as she turned to run away.

"Abigail Grace, that is no way to speak to your mother," I said as Abigail stomped down the hall.

This had turned into a royal mess. I'd explained to Abigail when she woke up that we needed to go back to our house. At first, she went along with it, but I must've given something away. I was trying so damn hard to hold it together and then she looked at me and asked, "We'll see Liam again, right? We can come back to the house, can't we?"

That's when I had to level with and explain to her that our time at the house and with Liam was over, but that we were lucky to have had it for a little while. But now it was time for us to go home, and it was time for Liam to move back to Austin.

Seeing those eyes well up with tears and her fighting to hold them back made me feel like the worst mother in the world, but I had to stay strong for Abigail. "Honey, I know this hurts. But we'll get back to our old routine and we'll have fun, you'll see," I promised her.

She was mostly silent on the way home, and while I was relieved not to have to answer any more questions, I was also worried. Abigail was rarely silent.

When we got back to the house, Abigail took her backpack and stomped back to her room. I fought back tears as I prayed for strength and guidance when, in reality, I wanted to sit down and bawl my eyes out. I'd fallen in love with him all over again, like an idiot. And now I'd broken both mine and my daughter's heart.

Nice job, Amber.

There was a knock on the door.

Perfect timing.

When I answered, my mother looked at me with alarm. "Amber? What happened?"

I shook my head, "You were right..."

She looked at me knowingly. "Liam?"

I nodded.

"Oh, sweetheart, I don't want to say I told you so..."

"Then don't," I said, as I quickly threw together a lunch for Abigail. It'd been early when we left Liam's, but she still had to go to school. Part of me was tempted to keep her home and have a bonding day with her, but the other part of me thought the routine might take her mind off the whole situation. Either way, it seemed like whatever decision I make would be wrong.

"Now Amber, there is no need to be cross. I told you once, and I'll tell you again. Liam Murphy is trouble, and he's all wrong for you."

Neither one of us had seen Abigail coming to stand at the mouth of the hallway, until we heard her voice call out, "You're wrong, he's perfect for us, he's perfect for mom."

"Now Abigail," my mother started gently, "I know it's hard to understand now, but sometimes things aren't meant to be."

"And sometimes they are. Liam is meant to be with us. Uncle Patrick said so."

That made me stop and my mom glanced at me, worried. "Abigail, honey, when did he tell you that?"

"When I was in the fairy garden the other day. But you couldn't let it happen. You had to ruin everything. Liam wanted us. He wouldn't have made us go—you were the one who made us go."

"Abigail, honey," I said, but she was already running away again, and I jumped when I heard her bedroom door slam behind her.

"Are you going to let her talk to you like that?"

I shook my head at my mother. " Of course not, but she's hurting right now, so I'm cutting her a little slack."

"Clearly, Liam has some hold over you two. I knew I was right to send him away. He should've stayed gone like I told him to," she said in a rush, then looked startled by her admission.

Everything in me stilled. "Come again?"

She was shaking her head. "It was nothing, just a slip..."

"It was a slip all right. What do you mean, you sent him away?"

She wouldn't meet my eyes, red staining her cheeks. "It was a long time ago, Amber."

"Not long enough. Now, tell me what you're talking about."

She finally met my eyes with fire in her own. "He was going to ruin your life. You were going to get out of this town and then suddenly you were telling me you and Liam were going to stay in Palmer and find work here, that you might not even go to college. I couldn't let you do that. I couldn't let you end up like me."

I huffed out a laugh. "Well guess what, Mom? He didn't stay, and I still ended up like you."

"Now Amber..."

"I mean, what were you thinking? Did you just tell him to scram? I don't understand."

She sighed, looking resigned. "No, I had a few frank conversations with him. He was very stubborn at first and kept insisting he could keep a roof over your head and take care of you. But Amber, I heard those promises before. Your dad was the same way. Cute and charming, but lazy with no drive. I didn't want that for you. It took some convincing, but I finally got him to see he would just bring you down. At least he cared enough to under-stand that. Once he did, it was easy to make him go."

I looked at her with my mouth hanging open as the full weight of her words sank in. Liam hadn't left me. He'd been chased away.

I gave her a grim smile then, "Ironic, isn't it, Mother? You wanted this grand life for me, and I still found a loser and ended up a single mom. And despite your low opinion of him, Liam would have never left his child."

"Maybe not, but he definitely wouldn't have been able to take care of you."

I barked out a laugh. "Oh, that's where you're wrong again, Mom. Turns out Liam is a covert Daddy Warbucks."

She laughed at the idea. "What are you talking about?"

That's when I filled her in on the conversation from this morning, when I found out about Liam's millionaire status, and how livid I was that he lied to me.

"I'm sorry what?" My mother asked in shock. "This might change things..."

I shook my head in disbelief. "It doesn't matter. He had every chance to tell me, but he hid it from me. I'm tired of things being hidden from me. First him, then Ethan, and now you, apparently. I don't know who to trust anymore. Evidently, I'm not smart enough to see what's right in front of me... turns out I've been surrounded by liars my whole life. The only person who hasn't lied to me is my daughter." I said, growing angrier with each word.

My mother approached me cautiously. "Sweetheart, I understand you're upset right now. I was doing what I thought was best for you. I never intended..."

"I get it, Mom. You thought you were doing the right thing, but it's still pretty fucked up," I said and she look shocked at my language. "I'm sorry. I can't think of a better word for it."

She looked away from me, tears in her eyes, but I didn't have it in me to comfort her. "Well, I'll take a cue from you and give you some space. When you calm down, we can talk about this more," she said, grabbing her purse and heading for the door. Before she opened it, however, she turned to me one last time and mumbled, "I truly want what's best for you, Amber, and I hate that I've caused you one ounce of pain. If nothing else, please believe that's true."

And with that, she was gone.

LIAM

O   ne thing that still needed to be done, regardless of what happened between me and Amber, was clearing out Pop's house. I had already brought my suitcases out. I would have to go back to Austin at some point, but I called Benny and told him he would have to put those fires out without me. There was too much at stake here at the moment.

I kept thinking about Amber's words. She felt like she needed to protect her daughter from me and her words hurt, even though I couldn't blame her.

I heard a knocking at the front door, and hope surged through me. Maybe she changed her mind. It didn't seem likely, but that didn't keep me from rushing to the front door and answering it without even checking who it was. A knot of dread replaced that hope when I saw Sandra standing on my doorstep.

"Hello Liam," she said cooly.

"Sandra," I replied curtly. "Sorry you came all this way, but I'm pretty sure we don't have anything to talk about," I said, not being able to handle her presence or her gloating. I started to close the door, but Sandra's words stopped me.

"She knows the truth now."

I opened the door, eyeing her suspiciously. "What truth are we talking about, exactly?"

Sandra sighed, looking away. "She knows I sent you away. She's furious with me and I'm not sure she'll ever talk to me again, but that doesn't mean I can't still try to make things right."

I felt like I was in a parallel universe. "What are you proposing?"

"I'm not letting you leave. It's obvious she loves you... that she always loved you. And as much as it pains me to be wrong, I have to believe if she still feels that way after all these years, then it's time for me to step out of the way."

"That's what I tried to tell you thirteen years ago," I reminded her, not being able to help myself.

She rolled her eyes. "Liam, I don't expect you to understand, but I thought I was doing what was best for my little girl. I felt so damn guilty that I couldn't give her a normal childhood with two parents, and I feared she was heading down the same path I'd gone down. I did what I felt I had to do to prevent her from making the same mistake. Then she'd met Ethan, and he'd come from a good family..."

"You mean rich?"

She had the decency to look ashamed. "I thought he would be able to take care of her, that she wouldn't have to suffer like I had. But I was wrong again."

I let out a heavy sigh. "Look Sandra, I know we're not each other's biggest fan, but even I can admit you did a great job raising Amber. Why can't you trust her to make her own decisions?"

"Fear is a tricky emotion, Liam. I can see now I was wrong. The least I can do is try to make it right, even if my daughter is upset with you. She told me about your little secret."

"And does that make me more appealing to you now?"

She glared at me. "I know I may seem like a money-grubbing witch to you, but all I wanted was my daughter to be well cared for. Now she's sitting in her house, with my sweet granddaughter, both of them heartbroken because you're no longer around. I don't know what your plans are, Liam, but I implore you to consider staying."

I shook my head. "Look, Sandra, I appreciate you coming all this way, but I don't think that's what Amber wants anymore. She made it clear she wasn't willing to risk her or Abigail's affections, and I have to respect her wishes, no matter how wrong I think she is."

Sandra put up her hands in a placating position. "Please... give it a little more time. Let the dust settle, maybe once she calms down..."

I swallowed hard. "Look, I'm not going anywhere this second. I still have to wrap up Pop's affairs, so I should be around for a little while longer."

She nodded. "Good, that's good... in the meantime, I'll see if I can't fix this mess."

"Oh, no, you don't. I think you need to let her make her own choices," I called after her.

She looked at me doubtfully. "Perhaps." Then she turned away and walked back primly to her car.

Never in my wildest dreams did I think Sandra would come apologizing to me—but it gave me hope. Maybe Amber would come to see I didn't mean any harm.

I blew out a long breath and looked towards the trees where the doves typically nested. "Pop, give me a sign here."

AMBER

After all the misery, I offered to keep Abigail home from school, but she declined. Despite my best efforts in trying to lure her out of her room, she refused to talk to me. I made her favorite dinner, and I put on her favorite movie, but she was unmoved, sitting on the seat with her arms crossed against her chest, looking at me coldly.

She never stayed mad at me for this long, but I couldn't blame her. I was pretty mad at myself, too.

All these years, I'd been placing the blame for my heartbreak squarely on Liam, never knowing my mother had played such a deceptive role in my misery. I couldn't decide if I was angrier at Liam for being convinced he could never be what I needed, or angrier with my mother for taking away my choice to love who I wanted.

I glanced at Abigail. I hoped I never felt so desperate that I'd take her choices away from her the way my mother did.

It was going to be some time before I could face her again.

When I tucked in Abigail that evening, she didn't want her stories, and she still didn't want to talk to me. I cried myself to sleep that night—it felt like I'd lost everybody I cared about.

The next morning, I took a still silent Abigail to school. As I pulled over in the drop-off line, I told her I loved her. Nada.

"Abigail, sweetheart," I said, "it's okay if you're mad at me, but after school today we're going to talk about what happened. We will work through this because that's what we do as a family—we don't shut one another out, okay?"

She glared up at me, but I could see a crack in her resolve, and it gave me hope. I leaned over and kissed her. "I love you more than anything. Remember that. Have a good day. I'll see you soon," I told her and watched miserably as she stomped off into the building.

I threw myself into working on my next group of orders, trying to figure out how I was going to approach this conversation with Abigail.

My mother called throughout the day, but I sent it to voicemail. I knew I wouldn't stay mad at her forever, but I wasn't ready to talk to her yet either. I still had to wrap my head around how I felt about all this now that I knew Liam hadn't meant to break his promise after all these years.

When it was time to pick up Abigail, I pushed those worries aside. My number one priority was my little girl, and everybody else would have to wait. But as I waited in line to pick her up, nobody came. I waited and waited and panic rose inside me.

"Stay calm, stay calm," I coached myself as I unbuckled my seatbelt and hurried out of the car into the front office of the school.

"Hi, I am Abigail's mom. She's usually out of school by now. Did her teacher say something about her staying behind?"

The attendance secretary looked at me, confused. "Her dad came by to get her earlier today."

At my look of horror, the secretary rushed to add, "he's still on her visitor's card. He's not on any forbidden list."

Oh my God.

"Ma'am?" the secretary questioned.

"Call the police. My daughter's been kidnapped."

I rushed to my car, took my phone out of the console and dialed 911. They patched me through to the sheriff, and I explained the situation. He knew Ethan hadn't been a part of Abigail's life.

Sheriff Graham tried to call me down. "Now Amber, I understand you're upset. But maybe he took her out for ice cream. Don't jump to the worst possible conclusion. We're sending cruisers out now to canvas the area. Please stay calm."

"I need to look for her," I said, but he reprimanded me gently.

"No. No, the best thing you can do is go home and wait. I know that's difficult, but someone should be there in case she shows up, okay?"

I hurried home and the first thing I did when I got there was search the house, hoping she was hiding in a corner somewhere, but the place was empty.

I released a primal scream. This couldn't be happening. I knew the sheriff thought maybe Ethan was just taking her out for a quick visit, but Ethan didn't do anything small and I recalled his angry declaration the last time I saw him—he would be in his daughter's life, whether I liked it or not. Now he was making good on that threat.

I couldn't sit here and wait. So I started making calls and the first person I dialed was Liam.

"Amber?" he answered hopefully.

"She's gone," I croaked out.

"What? Abigail?"

"Ethan came and got her out of school. She's gone."

"I'm on my way. Stay put," he said and hung up the phone.

Though Palmer was a small town, Patrick's house was on the outskirts, and it usually took a good fifteen minutes to get to my house—Liam was here in ten.

When he burst through the door without knocking, I ran to him and he pulled me into his arms and I couldn't stop sobbing. I went over what happened with him and I don't know how he understood me through all the crying, but he nodded emphatically.

"Okay," he said, trying to remain calm. "Sheriff Graham's right. You need to stay here in case she comes back. I'll go out and look for her, okay? In the meantime, call everybody you know and have them on the lookout for her." I was nodding furiously.

He started towards the door, then he stopped and gave me a kiss. "I'm gonna go get our girl back," he promised, and for the first time in a long time, I trusted him.

I continued my calls, starting with my mother and Lena. Within minutes, the whole town of Palmer was on alert that Abigail was missing. Most of them were familiar with Ethan and his car, so I hoped they wouldn't get far without being spotted. But the attendance secretary said Ethan picked her up several hours earlier, so I was terrified of how far they could have gotten.

My mother called me back and promised me we would find her soon, "I spoke to my neighbors and my neighbor's neighbors in the next four towns over. Everybody is on the lookout, sweetheart. We are going to find her. Don't you worry," she said all business, and I remembered how good my mother was in times of crisis.

"I don't know what I would do if I would lose her mom."

"You will not lose her, sweetheart. I'm on my way. Hang tight."

Despite everything, I was relieved when she showed up. I fought the urge to call Liam and check in, but I needed him focused, and I fought the urge to run out of the house and go look for her myself because everybody agreed I needed to stay put so I'd be here when she got home.

"Abigail, please be safe, please come home to me," I prayed repeatedly, as my mom held me in her arms and rocked me back and forth.

"It's going to be okay," she said in my ear.

Please God, please bring her back to me.

LIAM

It was heartwarming to see the residents of Palmer come out in droves, searching for Abigail, but anger quickly consumed me. If I ever got my hands on that son of a bitch ex-husband of Amber's, he wouldn't live long enough to regret seeing me.

I looked everywhere I could think of—all the places Abigail mentioned she liked, all the places I thought her jackass father might think to go, but found nothing. It was getting dark and I would need more than the flashlight on my phone to continue searching.

I phoned Amber to update her and let her know where I was headed next. "We're going to find her. Don't worry, baby, I'll bring her home to you. I'm gonna stop at the house and pick-up some supplies."

"Okay... Liam? Thank you."

"There's no need to thank me. I would do anything for you or Abigail. I love you both more than anything. She will not be taken away from us," I promised, not even thinking about the words as they rushed out of my mouth.

There was a brief silence and I could hear she was crying again. "Try to stay calm. That's the best thing we can do for her." I hung up the phone.

I raced home, certain none of the police would flag me down since they, along with everyone else, were looking for Abigail.

As my truck climbed the foothills into the mountains where Pop's house was, the sky went from mid-gray to inky black. Searchers would have to be careful out here at night. This is when the wolves like to come out.

As I pulled into my spot in front of the house and jumped out of my truck, I heard something peculiar—the doves were singing. They usually only did that in the mornings. My ears perked up at the noise and that's when I heard it: crying. It was muffled and soft. I stepped cautiously to my doorstep, and that's when I saw the familiar small head of curls. "Abigail?"

Her head jerked up. "Liam!" She launched from the porch into my arms.

I laughed, and she clung to me. "Are you okay? You gave us such a scare. What happened?"

She pulled her face from my neck to explain, "my daddy came and got me. At first, I was excited to see him, but then he said we were going to go far away and I was scared I would never see mommy again. So when we stopped at a gas station, I told him I had to use the bathroom and I ran. I ran to the closest place I knew was safe, your house. I'm sorry, I didn't know where else to go."

"Oh, no, don't be sorry, you came to the right place. I am so happy you're safe. Let's go find your mother immediately, she is worried sick—so is the rest of the town," I told her, depositing her into the passenger seat of my truck and hurrying to the driver's side where I cranked on the engine backing out of the spot and racing back into town.

Abigail looked up at me with worry. "Is Mom mad at me like I was with her?"

"I'm not sure I know what you mean."

"I told her I hated her after she made us leave your house. I didn't mean it... I was really sad we had to go. I thought we were going to stay together and be a family—that's what Uncle Patrick told me."

I looked at her curiously. "Pop told you that? When?"

"A few days ago, I was playing outside, and he whispered to me that mom and I were finally where we were supposed to be, with you."

A lump formed in my throat, and I didn't know whether I wanted to laugh or cry.

There you go again, Pop, meddling... thank you.

"Well, you see, your mom and I had a misunderstanding. It happens sometimes. We will work it out, but one thing that will never change is she loves you very much... and I love you, too."

As we pulled up to Amber's house and Abigail quickly unbuckled herself and hurled herself out of the truck, running up the stairs and through the door. I was hot on her heels when I saw her throw herself in the arms of an overjoyed Amber. They hugged and cried as Amber patted her head and told her she loved her repeatedly, and then she looked over Abigail's shoulder at me and whispered, "thank you."

Sandra got in the mix and hugged her granddaughter, as I quietly stepped away to let them have their moment.

Amber had been through a lot since I'd been gone, so I could understand her reluctance, but she was going to have to accept that I was here to stay, and we were going to be a family.

I would have the patience of a saint, if need be, but Amber would eventually realize we're supposed to be together. There's no way I'd let it be any other way now.

Sheriff Graham stopped by and asked Abigail a few questions. She relayed the same story she told me and he thanked her for her time. The search was called off, and the phone started ringing with well wishes and questions of whether they needed a casserole or a cake to tide them over after the rough afternoon. I had to laugh—I missed living in a small town.

While all of this was going on, I was texting Benny. I asked him to speak with our attorneys to draw up a purchase agreement and asked if he could help me ship my belongings to Palmer. I couldn't leave now—not even to pack up my things.

Upon hearing of the day's events, he happily agreed and told me he was on it, and promised he and Evie would visit soon.

After supper and bath, Abigail was out like a light, as was her grandmother. Amber smiled from the doorway at the sight of her mother draped over her daughter, and gently closed the door on the two sleeping.

She gave me a beckoning motion, and I followed her to the living room so we could talk. "Liam, I..."

"There's no need, Amber."

"No, when you called, you said you loved both of us and I guess... I guess I need to know if that was just said in the heat of the moment," she said.

"Are you kidding me? I never stopped loving you, and I think it only took me two minutes to fall in love with Abigail. That love is here to stay, and so am I."

She raised her eyebrows in question.

"I've been texting Benny while you were getting everything sorted. Our lawyers are going to sort out the purchase of the business, and he's going to pack up my stuff and ship it here. There's no way I'm leaving Palmer, not without the two of you... I'm rooted here now."

A brilliant smile stretched across her lips. "You really are something, you know that?"

I laughed. "I think I'm supposed to be telling you that."

"Liam, I'm sorry I doubted you for so long."

"You had no reason to think anything different."

"Yeah, but since you've been here, you've only proven to be trustworthy and reliable, and I still couldn't trust what I was feeling for you. There's a lot of baggage I need to sort through, but I took it out on you, and that wasn't fair."

"You were trying to protect your daughter, so it was more than fair. Just so you know, even if you decide you're not ready for me, I'm not going anywhere. I will wait as long as it takes..."

Then she was kissing me, her hand cupping my jaw firmly. I could taste the salt of her tears. Then she leaned back, smiling. "It's going to take about that long. Is that okay with you?"

I grinned at her then, "That's more than okay with me."

"And Liam, I need you to understand something else, too. What you told me about your business, it doesn't matter to me. I don't want anything to do with it, actually. I don't want you to feel obligated to take care of us."

"Well, too bad, because that's exactly what's happening. And I don't feel like I have to, but it is my job."

Frustration lit in her eyes. "That right there—that's what I'm talking about. I don't want you to feel like we're a job."

"Amber, let me say it another way. I mean, it's my job to take care of the people I love, and I love you and Abigail. I would do anything for you both."

I could see her physically swallowing back her tears. "I love you, Liam. I never stopped," she whispered, reaching for me.

I pulled her into my arms again. "I love you too. I hate that it took me this long to come back to you, but I'm grateful for the interference."

She looked at me with confusion. "Interference?"

"Right. I forgot to tell you. It started with some dove s..."

Epilogue

Six months later...

We couldn't have asked for a better day for a backyard wedding. Patrick's backyard was filled with our nearest and dearest, smiling and clapping for us as Liam and I pledged our love for eternity.

Liam and I looked out from our bedroom window as we changed into our honeymoon clothes. Our guests were still milling about, talking as they waited for the new bride and groom to come out to blow bubbles. Abigail was very insistent that rice not be thrown because it could hurt the doves.

I smiled at the sight of the fairy lights in the trees and the wildflowers in the brush. Those were the same wildflowers I had twined into a garden halo for Abigail's hair when she walked down the aisle. She'd served as both flower girl and maid of honor, and after Liam and I had pledged our love to one another, Abigail joined us and we all pledged our love to one another as a family.

This day had been a long time coming, even though our engagement had been fairly short. A lot had happened in the last six months.

Abigail and I moved into Patrick's old house, which was now our house. It appeared a family would get to enjoy the space after all, just as Patrick had wanted.

I opened my cake shop, Cakes on Main, last month and Liam convinced me to go big with the marque sign. It's the most talked about—and visited—storefront in town.

On a more sinister note, Ethan was arrested for attempted kidnapping of Abigail. In a plot twist even I didn't see coming, he was also wanted for bank fraud, among other financial crimes. It turns out he came back to Palmer not because he was interested in being a family man, but because he was hoping to cash in on some of the money I was making and figured he could use Abigail as a pawn.

I almost felt sorry for the guy... almost.

I thought explaining the situation to Abigail would be difficult, but she seemed undisturbed by the news. She loved her father, but he'd never been a part of her life, and as she'd told me, "That's okay. That's why Liam is here. He's supposed to be my dad."

I couldn't argue with her logic, and I suspect that was exactly why Liam was here. He was supposed to be ours, and now he officially was.

"What are you smiling about?" Liam asked, coming from behind me and wrapping his arms around my middle. "Everything, but mainly my new husband," I told him over my shoulder.

"I can't believe all of this is ours," he said into my ear. "I never imagined you would be mine again, hell I never imagined I have a daughter, or any kids after you and I split up."

"It's funny how quickly things change. Now you're a married man with a daughter."

"That's right, and I couldn't imagine it getting any better than this."

I turned in his arms then and looked up into that handsome face rising on my toes to kiss him. "Well, now that you're a father of one, I'm going to need you to wrap your head around being a father of two."

He jerked back. "Say what now?" I smiled at him. "For real?" He asked, grinning.

I nodded, trying to choke back my tears.

He pulled me into his arms, kissing me passionately. "Thank you for making me a dad... again."

This was the fairytale we had dreamed about since we were kids. It just took a little longer to find us than we originally planned.

THE END

Thank you for reading **Rebuilding Forever.**

If you liked this book, then you will love *Running Towards You*!

Why you'll love it...

* Retired NFL football player
* Runaway Bride
* Best Friend's Brother
* Next Door Neighbor
* Off Limits
* Second Chance
* Grumpy/Protective Hero

Here's a sneak peek...

Haley Ellis. My first love—no, scratch that—the love of my life.

And for one steamy summer, she was mine.

When summer ended, she abruptly broke things off and walked away, leaving a hole where my future used to be.

Now she's back in Hanalei, the sleepy surf town where we used to spend summers as kids.

She's still fierce, still fiery, and still my little sister's best friend.

I've made my home in Hanalei as a surf instructor after a career-ending knee injury.

And she was supposed to be getting married...

So why is she sunbathing on the adjoining porch, making my blood boil with desire?

I want to be angry with her for ruining our happily ever after.

But the pain in her eyes ignites my protective instincts.

Now she's reaching for me, not just for safety, but for the love we left unfinished.

Can we survive the second wave of love, or will this be our final wipeout?

Scan HERE to get your copy!

Haley Ellis. My first love—no, scratch that—the love of my life. And for one steamy summer, she was mine.

When summer ended, she abruptly broke things off and walked away, leaving a hole where my future used to be.

Now she's back in Hanalei, the sleepy surf town where we used to spend summers as kids.

She's still fierce, still fiery, and still my little sister's best friend.

I've made my home in Hanalei as a surf instructor after a career-ending knee injury.

And she was supposed to be getting married...

So why is she sunbathing on the adjoining porch, making my blood boil with desire?

I want to be angry with her for ruining our happily ever after.

But the pain in her eyes ignites my protective instincts.

Now she's reaching for me, not just for safety, but for the

love we left unfinished.

Can we survive the second wave of love, or will this be our final wipeout?

Scan HERE to get your copy!

HALEY

I tried to take in another deep, cleansing breath—they had to work at some point, right? At some point, I shouldn't want to run screaming from my own wedding.

This is ridiculous. I'm sure Marcus must be having some of the same jitters as I was having. We should talk it out and then I could walk down the aisle to him, certain of my decision.

I started for the door, having to make broad movements to account for the overly full tulle skirt of my wedding dress. This was not the dress I would have chosen for myself. In fact, most elements of the wedding were not things I would have chosen for us. But with Marcus being in the public eye as the up-and-coming star of congress, he insisted the wedding planner make all the decisions because she would know exactly what was expected of a rising politician who had aspirations for the White House.

Thus, everything was cream and beige. I still shivered at that last color and so did my best friend and maid of honor, Tess, considering she got stuck with the dowdy beige number that made her to-die-for curves look like a sack of potatoes.

"Um, excuse me. Where do you think you're going?" the wedding planner, Nadia said in a slightly shrill voice.

I couldn't wait until I no longer had to hear that voice. "I just need to have a quick word with Marcus…"

"Oh no, no, no, you can't be serious? It's bad luck for him to see you before the ceremony," she said, as if I were the stupidest person she'd ever met.

I let out a strained laugh. "That's a superstition," I started, but Nadia wasn't having it.

"That may be so, but it's been proven accurate time and time again…" she continued as my eyes darted to Tess, who was standing behind Nadia, watching me carefully.

She saw my look of panic and interceded, physically stepping in between Nadia and me. "Nadia, I'm so sorry to interrupt, but is that ice sculpture supposed to look like an angel peeing?"

"What? Oh my God, not again," Nadia huffed, grabbing a walkie-talkie from her waistband and angrily barking out orders as she hurried from the room, Tess following behind her mouthing the words 'you're welcome' as she cleared the path for my exit.

I hustled out of the bridal suite and down the hall to the opposite end of the building towards the groom's suite. Marcus was so pragmatic, his calm and no-nonsense approach to life always assured me there was a plan in place. I needed to hear his practical reasoning now before I made the biggest commitment of my life.

I knocked on the door and slowly opened it at the same time. It wasn't like Marcus and I had anything to hide from one another, and I didn't have time for manners at that moment.

"Marcus," I started, but my voice caught in my throat at the sight that met my eyes. I was staring at the back of Marcus, hunched over his trusty assistant, Skylar. He had his tux on, but his pants were down around his knees as his hips pumped furiously into a moaning Skylar.

They both stilled. Then he turned to look at me. "This is not what it looks like," he said almost instantly.

I don't know why, but I laughed. Maybe because what he said was so absurd, though it seemed to be an odd time to even note that. "I may have been born in the dark, Marcus, but I wasn't born yesterday. I can see exactly what you're doing."

There was a shuffling as he and Skylar parted and covered their necessary bits. Skylar looked between the two of us, then fled the room like a scared rabbit. I couldn't explain the feelings that were coursing through me. I should be enraged. I should be sad, but I mostly felt... numb.

I looked at him awkwardly, "I—I'll let you fix yourself up, and then we should talk," I said, turning around and closing the door behind me.

My reaction puzzled me. It wasn't like in the movies, where the woman started throwing things or dropped to her knees in agony. None of that felt like the right thing to do.

I stood outside the door, looking through the window on the opposite side of the hall unseeingly for a couple of minutes before I heard the door open behind me and Marcus cleared his throat.

"First of all," he said calmly, "I'm sorry you had to see that." And I laughed again. He said it as if I had just walked in on him masturbating, not like he'd been fucking his trashy assistant mere minutes before our wedding ceremony.

"I know it's no excuse, but I'm nervous. This is a big event, and I realize you have every right to be upset, but I just ask that..." He wavered, then forged ahead, "that we table this until after the ceremony."

I felt my mouth drop open, but he wasn't done. "Haley, we have a lot of guests waiting out there for us who have given up their precious time to see us get married. We don't want to disappoint them. I know this must have been shocking to you, but I am confident we can work through it... just not right now," he said diplomatically, as if he was talking to a political pundit.

That's when the anger finally hit in full force.

"Are you fucking kidding me?"

His eyes widened, and he looked to each end of the hall to spot any passersby. "Haley," he chastised, "lower your voice."

"The hell I will!"

He sighed as if he was dealing with a petulant child. "Haley, look, I understand you're upset, and we definitely need to have a conversation about what just happened. But you can't tell me this one little indiscretion is going to ruin everything we have worked so hard to build... or this beautiful day with all the guests who are here waiting for us at this very moment," he reasoned.

None of it made sense to me—not a damn word, and yet, I was nodding my head.

I hated to disappoint anybody, and later I would remember this moment and think I must have been in such shock that I didn't know what else to do.

I never used to be like this. I was decisive and trusted my instincts. But now, even small decisions were scary and potentially life-altering, and I often found myself second-guessing everything.

"Come on, Haley," he said. "You know I love you. My nerves got the better of me. That's all that you saw in there. It was purely physical. I could never feel the same way about her as I do about you," he said. "This is the most important day of our lives, and I know I fucked up, but please don't let it ruin everything. Let's be sensible about this."

Marcus was right about one thing. This was the most important day of our lives together, and it would not do to act rashly. Later, I would blame that reasoning as

I nodded and turned to head back towards the bridal suite.

Nadia was there, directing everybody into position, and Tess was by my side.

The one thing I had insisted on was that she be the one to walk me down the aisle since my parents were gone. Nadia and Marcus both balked because it was against tradition, but I would not yield.

She'd been my best friend for most of my life, and I wanted her by my side on this important day. I stepped in stride next to Tess, and she looked at me with a worried expression. "Haley? What happened?"

I shook my head, "I... I don't quite know yet."

The other bridesmaids were heading out in front of me, half of which weren't even friends of mine but acquaintances of Marcus'. He appointed them to these positions because he thought it would curry favor for him later.

Nadia was busy barking orders as Tess grabbed my elbow and yanked me back. "Haley? If you don't want to do this, you don't have to, no questions asked."

Her gentle reminder made tears prick at the back of my eyes. Or maybe the reality of what I'd just seen hit me. I blinked them away, not wanting to mess up my makeup, and gave her a watery smile. "Thank you, Tess."

She looked at me seriously. "Don't forget the code word," she said, and I bit back a smile before Nadia snapped at us to face forward and start heading toward the alcove before the aisle.

Tess and I had met when we were twelve at our parents' respective vacation homes in Hanalei, Hawaii. We became instant friends and navigated those awkward summers as preteens and teenagers together. Anytime we got in an awkward situation or one of us wanted out because of impending embarrassment, we had a codeword. Either of us could say it, no questions asked, and the other was required to get us out of the situation. Even though it was the silliest code word we could conjure up in our twelve-year-old brains, we never changed it.

The wedding march started, and I clutched at Tess's hand. "Haley," she said in a tense whisper, "you're scaring me."

I shook my head. "Don't be silly, there's nothing to be scared of," I said as we drifted to the mouth of the aisle.

I looked down the aisle. Everybody was standing and watching me intently, smiling at the radiant bride. Little did they know I was fighting the urge to throw up.

My eyes traveled down the aisle and met Marcus', and he gave me that smile... the same smarmy smile he gave TV reporters. I'd never cared for that look, but I told myself he only did that for the camera. But now, as far as he was concerned, he was on camera, and I would only get the camera-ready version of him. No love for me or excitement over what we were about to do, no remorse for what he'd done, no acknowledgment of it at all, in fact.

I looked over at Tess, panicking, and whispered the too-long ago, pinky-promised code word to her. "Dick weasel."

She looked over at me with wide eyes. "Really?" Then she looked at the crowd, smiling.

"Yes, really. Dick weasel! Dick weasel!" I said, my voice rising.

The guests murmured quietly to one another, looking confused, and Marcus gave me a questioning look as Tess said in my ear. "Shit, Haley, I don't know how to get us out of here," before she sucked in a deep breath and said, "Fuck it! Let's run!"

Tess and I looked at each other, and then I hiked my skirt over my elbow. She grabbed my hand, and we ran out of there as fast as possible.

I registered the murmurs rising to a crescendo with the guests, the shrill voice of Nadia behind me asking me what the hell I thought I was doing. But at no time did I ever hear Marcus call for me.

We ran straight out of that church and into the waiting limo that was supposed to be whisking Marcus and me away after the ceremony to drop us off at The Lane, where we would have the reception.

Instead, the driver looked confused at me and Tess, who was still panting. "Where to, ladies?"

I looked over at Tess with raised eyebrows. "Umm..."

She shrugged, and I blurted out, "Driver, get us to the airport as quickly as you can."

That's how I ended up in the airport ticket line in a poofy wedding dress with my best friend by my side, making plans on the fly. "I'll get you some clothes at the duty-free shop. What are you going to do with this monstrosity?"

"I don't know... hock it," I added bitterly.

Tess shook her head. "I wish there was time for you to tell me what happened, but you have to promise to fill me in as soon as you land. In the meantime, after I see you off here, I'm going straight to your apartment to start packing up your things. I'll send as much as I can to Hanalei."

"I can't believe I'm doing this. I haven't been to Hanalei since before mom and dad..." I trailed off.

"I wish I could get on that plane with you," she said, but I knew that wasn't possible.

Tess was a registered nurse, and she couldn't drop everything at a moment's notice and skip town. People were counting on her. I was an elementary school art teacher, and it was summer break, so I had some time to hide away, which is what I intended to do.

I didn't want to confront Marcus, and I certainly didn't want to answer any of the reporters who wanted to know what happened between the congressional boy wonder and his runaway bride. I didn't want to hear his lame excuses about why I should forgive his indiscretion. More than that, I needed to stop and figure out why I was about to commit myself to a man who would cheat on me minutes before we were to be married, but also who I had so few feelings for.

When I looked down that aisle at him, a thought occurred to me. It should have broken my heart to see him with Skylar, but my thought was, "Well, that makes sense."

Skylar was his right hand, by his side at all times. She understood all the political gibberish he went on about and was actually interested in it. It just made sense—a lot more sense than me and him.

When it was my turn at the ticket counter, I ordered a one-way ticket to the island of Kauai. From there, I would rent a car and drive to the bungalow my parents and I stayed at every summer. The place where I had so many fond memories, and also where I experienced my biggest heartbreak—even bigger than the one I was going through now.

It didn't matter anymore, I told myself. What mattered was getting away from all this noise and my duplicitous life.

I kissed a tearful Tess goodbye and promised to call her as soon as I landed to give her all the awful details.

Then I was collecting my ticket and finding the nearest duty-free shop where I bought a pair of sweats, and an 'I love California' t-shirt. I asked the cashier for an extra big bag so I could stuff that god-awful wedding dress into it. The wedding dress was the only luggage I had, and I unceremoniously stuffed it into the overhead compartment after I boarded.

I had nothing but time to think as I made my way to Hanalei. I thought mostly about how I allowed myself to get into this situation and how I lost control over my life.

Marcus was an insensitive, cheating bastard, but I was guilty of a much bigger sin—I had given up on myself. I tamped down the real Haley, her wants and desires, and did everything in my power to mold myself into someone he wanted. I couldn't blame Marcus for that, no matter how much he got wrong.

Truth be told, I had given up on myself the moment I gave Cooper up.

Scan HERE to get your copy!